George E. Stevens

The Queen City in 1869

The City of Cincinnati

George E. Stevens

The Queen City in 1869
The City of Cincinnati

ISBN/EAN: 9783337327491

Printed in Europe, USA, Canada, Australia, Japan

Cover: Foto ©Andreas Hilbeck / pixelio.de

More available books at **www.hansebooks.com**

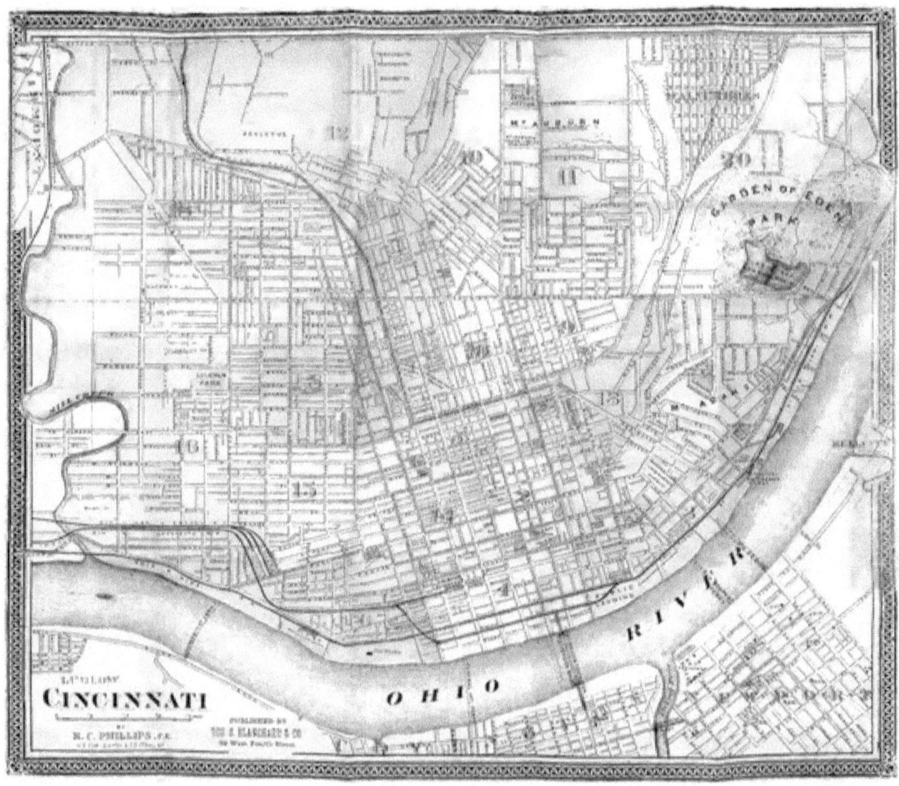

GARDEN OF EDEN PARK
OHIO RIVER
CINCINNATI
BY
M. C. PHILLIPS
PUBLISHED BY
GEO. E. BLANCHARD & CO

THE

CITY OF CINCINNATI:

A Summary

OF ITS

ATTRACTIONS, ADVANTAGES, INSTITUTIONS, AND
INTERNAL IMPROVEMENTS,

WITH

A Statement of its Public Charities.

BY

GEO. E. STEVENS.

CINCINNATI:
GEO. S. BLANCHARD & CO.,
NO. 39 WEST FOURTH STREET.
1869.

PUBLISHERS' NOTICE.

CINCINNATI, the largest inland city of the United States—the center of trade of the Ohio Valley, with a population of over a quarter of a million, admirable location and climate, and suburbs unequaled in beauty by those of any city in the world—has recently had no publication setting forth its attractions and advantages, both as a place of trade and residence. This want, it is hoped, has now been supplied.

The publishers have borne in mind the impatience of the public toward prolixity in style, and, at the risk of omitting valuable material, have endeavored to present, *to be read*, a compend, stating, in the most concise terms, only the leading features which characterize the great city of the Central West. The original design included full descriptions of the suburbs, but the limits of the volume forbade these. As it now is, the book, without being a mere tabular guide, will be a manual of great service to every stranger. The publishers bespeak for it the attention of every merchant, manufacturer, and property-holder in Cincinnati, confident that such a publication will be a powerful agent in the advancement of their interests. Believing in the promise of a magnificent future for the Queen City, they issue this volume, trusting that no citizen will be ashamed to declare it a fair exponent of the great metropolis of the Ohio Valley.

PREFACE.

THE design of this volume has been to present, in the briefest possible terms, a summary of the attractions and advantages, and to assert the rightful sovereignty, of the Queen City. Not a history, recording the past, but rather a photograph, an instantaneous fixing of the present, has been intended. With this aim, taxing the utmost skill to develop the salient features—to properly adjust the effects of light and shade—to select just the point of best perspective—the difficulty has been to determine, not what to insert, but what to omit, not how much, but how little to say. Thus the work, while partly the result of compilation, has required, in its preparation, much time and labor. It is submitted in the firm belief that those who have attempted a task similar to this, will form the most charitable opinions of its execution. Entire freedom from inaccuracies is not claimed. The nature of the contents will account for the appearance of matter which may have ceased since it was written, to represent facts correctly.

Reference has been had to various sources for information, among which are to be credited the daily papers of the city, especially the *Gazette*, and the volumes of the late Charles Cist, to whose labors Cincinnati has been so greatly indebted. That invaluable work, "Lippincott's Gazetteer," has supplied important items. In the preparation of the statement of the charities of the city, free use has been made of published reports of the various institutions. To the "Atlantic Monthly," acknowledgment is also due.

The most valuable part of the book will be found to be the chapter upon the growth and future of Cincinnati. This is from the pen of E. D. Mansfield, Esq., and will command the attention and confidence which it deserves.

G. E. S.

CINCINNATI, *April* 20, 1869.

CONTENTS.

THE QUEEN CITY.

CINCINNATI, entering in 1869 the ninth decade of its existence, is the largest and wealthiest inland city of America. The number of its inhabitants is estimated at over a quarter of a million. Settled in 1788, one hundred and seven years after Philadelphia, it has to-day a population as great as that city contained in 1840, and equal to that of New York in 1833. Receiving early in its history the title "Queen City of the West," it has never lost its claim to that proud eminence. Its present greatness may well excite contemplation, and its citizens gather thence a fresh energy to stimulate a future growth, the limit of which none can place. It has been no idle fancy that has styled Cincinnati "the Paris of America." Already the great workshop and exchange of the populous Valley of the Ohio, a territory greater in area than the whole of France, Nature has bestowed gifts which need only the seconding of Art to develop upon the banks of "La Belle Riviere" the grandest and most beautiful city of the New World. American brain and nerve and muscle will find here a center where the facilities for the creation of wealth shall be inferior only to those for its enjoyment. Inevitably Cincinnati, the metropolis of the fairest portion of the United States, is moving steadily and compactly forward to a magnificent future. Its commercial supremacy was and is "manifest destiny," while natural advantages belong to it which leave it few rivals in beauty of situation among the cities of the world.

The Cincinnati of A. D. 1900 will display to the visitor its vast commerce and manufactures crowding its lower plateau, while upon the elevation of the surrounding hills shall stretch away for miles under the genial skies of this favored region the dwellings of its inhabitants. Pushing its limits far out on every side, there will be, at no distant period, one consolidated municipality, gathering into its embrace one after another the now suburban villages, until one and the same boundary shall mark the limit of the city and the county in which it is situate.

In the recently-uttered words of a distinguished citizen, the Cincinnati of the not remote future is to be "a city fair to the sight, with a healthy public spirit, and high intelligence sound to the core; a city with pure water to drink, pure air to breathe, spacious public grounds, wide avenues; a city not merely of much traffic, but of delightful homes; a city of manufactures, wherein is made every product of art—the needle-gun, the steam-engine, the man of learning, the woman of accomplishment; a city of resort for the money profit of its dealings, and the mental and spiritual profit of its culture—the Edinboro' of a new Scotland, the Boston of a new New England, the Paris of a new France."

Most justly has one of the ablest of American political economists said, that "it requires no keenness of observation to perceive that Cincinnati is destined to become the focus and mart for the grandest circle of manufacturing thrift on this continent. Her delightful climate, her unequaled and ever-increasing facilities for cheap and rapid commercial intercourse with all parts of the country and the world, her enterprising and energetic population, her own elastic and exulting youth, are all elements which predict and insure her electric progress to giant greatness. It may be doubted if there is another spot on earth where food, fuel, cotton, timber, and iron can all be concentrated so cheaply as here. Such fatness of soil, such a wealth of mineral treasure—coal, iron, salt, and the finest clays for all purposes of use—and all cropping out from the steep, facile banks of placid, though not sluggish, navigable rivers. How many El Dorados could equal this valley of the Ohio?"

CHAPTER II.

LOCATION—PHYSICAL CHARACTERISTICS—LA BELLE
RIVIERE—GENERAL DESCRIPTION.

THE City of Cincinnati, the county seat of Hamilton County, State of Ohio, is situated in a valley of circular form, about twelve miles in circumference, which is bisected by the Ohio River passing through it in a course from north-east to south-west. The city rests upon the north bank; and, lying opposite, in the State of Kentucky, are the towns of Dayton, Ludlow, and Brooklyn, and the cities of Newport and Covington. The Licking River empties into the Ohio between the cities just mentioned. The hills surrounding the city form a natural amphitheater unequaled in beauty upon this continent. From their summits, varying in height from three to four hundred feet, may be seen the splendid panorama of the great river and three cities with all their busy life. While Philadelphia, New Orleans, Chicago, Buffalo, and St. Louis are built on comparatively level ground, and afford scarcely any noticeable variety of position, the site of Cincinnati is one upon which the eye of taste may rest with admiration, while the natural advantages of location, which the city and its environs present, seize the attention of every beholder.

The river front of the city is about ten miles in length, and the northern line over two miles from low-water mark.

The greater part of the city is built on two terraces, or plateaus—the first, fifty feet above low-water mark, and the second one hundred and eight feet. The front margin of the latter plateau, originally a steep bank, has been graded to a gentle declivity, so that the drainage of much of the city is made directly into the river. This upper terrace, comprising two-thirds of the area of the valley, is somewhat undulating in its surface, but in the main slopes to the north, and, at an average distance of a mile, terminates at the base of the hills.

The central and business portions of the city are compactly built. The streets are laid out with regularity, and are about sixty-six feet in width. The sidewalks are wide, and paved with brick and stone. Shade trees adorn many of the streets and avenues. Main Street runs almost due north from the river, with Broadway, Sycamore, Walnut, Vine, Race, Elm, Plum, Central Avenue, and others, parallel with it. These are intersected at right angles by streets running east and west, and mostly deriving their names from their relative po-

sition—Front, Second, Pearl, Third, Fourth, Fifth, etc.
The principal streets for wholesale business are Main,
Walnut, Vine, Second, and Pearl; for retail, Fourth,
Fifth, and Central Avenue. At the foot of Main, Sycamore, and Broadway, on Front Street, is the Public
Landing, an open area of ten acres, with one thousand
feet front. The shore is paved from low-water mark,
and furnished with floating wharves which rise and fall
with the river. Cincinnati is remarkable for solidity
of appearance, and presents a striking appearance both
in regard to the architecture and the magnitude of its
buildings. The material generally employed for the
fronts of the best buildings is a fine freestone or sandstone, though white limestone is used to a considerable
extent.

The city was settled in 1788, and incorporated as a
city in 1819. In 1800, it contained only seven hundred
and fifty inhabitants. For several years after its first
settlement, it suffered greatly from Indian ravages.
When this source of danger ceased, the new city moved
forward to greatness with rapid strides. The accompanying engraving represents Cincinnati as it appeared
in 1802.

The Ohio River, which curves so gracefully around
the southern margin of the city, is one of the finest
rivers in the world. The early French adventurers
called it "La Belle Riviere"—the Beautiful River.

CINCINNATI IN 1802.

This, it is stated, is the signification of the Indian appellation Ohio. No river on the globe rolls for so great a distance in such uniform, smooth, and placid current. It is formed by the confluence of the Alleghany and Monongahela in the western part of Pennsylvania. Flowing in a south-westerly direction, and dividing Ohio, Indiana, and Illinois, on the right, from Virginia and Kentucky, on the left, it empties into the Mississippi about one hundred and seventy-five miles below St. Louis. The entire length of the river is upward of nine hundred and fifty miles, and of the valley, not following the windings of the stream, about six hundred and fourteen miles. The principal tributaries are the Muskingum, Great Kanawha, Big Sandy, Scioto, Miami, Green, Kentucky, Wabash, Cumberland, and Tennessee. At Pittsburgh, its elevation above the level of the sea is six hundred and eighty feet; at the entrance of the Muskingum, five hundred and forty-one feet; at the mouth of the Scioto, four hundred and sixty-four feet; opposite Cincinnati, four hundred and fourteen feet; at its confluence with the Mississippi, three hundred and twenty-four feet—making the average descent less than five inches to the mile. The current is very gentle, being about three miles per hour. The velocity is, of course, very much increased at high water. In common with other Western rivers, the Ohio is subject to great elevations and depressions. The average range between high and low water is about fifty feet; but in a few instances, as in 1832, the rise has been over sixty feet. The navigable waters of the Ohio and its tributaries are estimated at not less than five thousand miles, and the extent of area drained at two hundred and twenty thousand square miles. Descending the river from Pittsburgh, the scenery is highly picturesque and beautiful. The hills, two and three hundred feet high, and intervening valleys, approach the stream on either side. These exhibit in the spring and early summer a bounteous wealth of verdure, and in autumn all the glories of color which have made the forests of the West so justly celebrated. The graceful curves and bends of the river, exhibiting in the distance one range of hills gliding into another, with their beautifully-rounded summits, produce a series of splendid views rarely found.

Cincinnati is in longitude 84° 26′ west from Greenwich, and latitude 39° 6′ 30″ north. The upper terrace of the city is five hundred and forty feet above the level of the sea.

The surface of the river at low water is four hundred and thirty-one feet, and that of the surrounding hills about eight hundred and fifty feet, above the sea. The summit of Mount Adams is three hundred and ninety-six feet above low-water mark in the Ohio River, Mount Auburn four hundred and fifty-nine feet, and Mount

Harrison, west of the city, four hundred and sixty feet.

Geologically, Cincinnati is situated in the lower Silurian formation. Sand and gravel underlie the greater portion of the city. The adjacent region furnishes, in inexhaustible quantities, a blue fossiliferous limestone, which is a most valuable building material.

Situated in the heart of a rich and populous district, through which are scattered rapidly-growing cities and towns, Cincinnati is the commercial metropolis of several of the finest States in the Union. Of the region between Lake Erie and Tennessee River, and between Baltimore and Saint Louis, comprising the fairest part of North America, it is the center.

A table of distances to important points, by water and by railway, is here given:

BY RIVER.

	Miles.
Aurora, Ind.,	26
Cairo,	529
Carrolton, Ky.,	81
Evansville, Ind.,	337
Guyandotte, Va.,	165
Ironton, O.,	144
Lawrenceburg, Ind.,	22
Louisville,	142
Madison, Ind.,	91
Marietta, O.,	306
Maysville, Ky.,	61

Miles.

Memphis,	781
New Albany, Ind.,	145
New Orleans,	1520
Parkersburg, Va.,	293
Pomeroy, O.,	220
Pittsburgh,	476
Portsmouth, O.,	114
St. Louis,	708
Vicksburg,	1128
Wheeling,	382

BY RAIL.

Altoona, Pa.,	430
Baltimore,	580
Boston,	936
Buffalo,	438
Cairo,	396
Chicago,	280
Cleveland,	255
Columbus, O.,	120
Dayton,	60
Detroit,	267
Evansville, Ind.,	243
Harrisburg, Pa.,	562
Indianapolis,	115
Lexington, Ky.,	100
Louisville,	105
Marietta, O.,	196
Memphis,	514
Nashville,	330
New Orleans,	890
New York,	744
Philadelphia,	668

	Miles.
Pittsburgh,	313
Richmond, Ind.,	70
St. Louis,	340
Springfield, O.,	84
Toledo,	202
Urbana,	95
Vincennes,	194
Vicksburg,	752
Washington,	610
Xenia, O.,	65

Cincinnati, already distinguished for regularity and beauty of streets, is susceptible, by reason of its peculiar topographical features, of improvements of this kind, which will leave it without a rival among American cities. Large foresight is being displayed in the engineering of public improvements. Splendid avenues and parks are being projected and constructed, rendering it certain that no Baron Haussman will be needed in the next century to remodel the Queen City.

CHAPTER III.

The Stranger in Cincinnati—Approach—General Directions—Different Quarters of the City—Suspension Bridge—Prospects from the Hills—Suburbs—Public Buildings and Points of Interest.

THE stranger arriving in Cincinnati will find little difficulty in acquainting himself with the streets and avenues of the city, and making his way to any part without trouble. The map of the city will aid him to get the points of the compass, and give a general idea of the location. It will also indicate the relative position of the railroad depots, principal hotels, the post-office, etc. The city is very compact, and communication between the different points is easy. The lines of street cars afford a speedy transit from the railroad depots to the vicinity of excellent hotels. The hack rates of Cincinnati were established before the war, and have never since been altered. As they are not now observed by any one, they are not here given. The best plan is to have a distinct understanding with the hackman before entering his carriage. The railroad omnibus lines are well managed, and transport passengers and baggage with great celerity. The streets running north and south are numbered from the river north; the east and west streets, each way from Main Street.

The leading hotels of the city are here mentioned:

BURNET HOUSE.—This spacious hotel is located on the corner of Third and Vine Streets. Its fame is known throughout the United States. Its splendid appointments and excellent management will continue to perpetuate its celebrity. The building is in the Italian style of architecture, and has a front of two hundred and twelve feet on Third Street and two hundred and ten feet on Vine Street. The present proprietors are Messrs. A. C. Joslin & Co.

GIBSON HOUSE.—This well-known and popular hotel is on Walnut Street, west side, between Fourth and Fifth. Its location is central and convenient to all the lines of street cars. Directly opposite are the Merchant's Exchange and the Young Men's Mercantile Library. Its interior arrangements are admirable, and the convenience and comfort of guests are unceasingly consulted. Never has this house been more attractive or prosperous than under the management of Messrs. Sinks, Corré & Co., its present lessees.

SPENCER HOUSE.—This house needs no introduction to those at all acquainted with Cincinnati. It is on the north-west corner of Broadway and the Public Landing.

It has long been a favorite with travelers on the river
and guests from all parts of the South. The internal
arrangements are unsurpassed in their elegance and
convenience. The requirements of light and ventilation are well met, and the prospect upon the river and
the Kentucky adjacencies is a splendid one. This
house is now conducted by Messrs. Sweny & Drown.

ST. JAMES HOTEL.—This house, which has won in
the few years of its existence an enviable reputation, is
located on Fourth Street, at the corner of Hammond
Street, east of Main Street. This is the only hotel
upon this fashionable promenade. Its facilities for the
entertainment of guests are admirable, and no house
has gained friends more rapidly than this under the
popular management of Henry P. Elias, Esq.

WALNUT STREET HOUSE, as its name indicates, is
on Walnut Street, at the corner of Gano, between Sixth
and Seventh Streets. It covers ten thousand square feet
of ground. The dining room is a magnificent apartment. The parlors are spacious and elegant, and all the
rooms are of convenient size and arrangement. There
are few pleasanter places of abode for the stranger in
the city. Messrs. Pratt & Davis, its present owners, are
gentlemen who thoroughly understand their business.
Colonel Pratt was for a long time proprietor of the
Spencer House of this city.

MERCHANTS HOTEL.—This house has always been a

favorite with visitors to Cincinnati. It is located on Fifth Street, east of Main. It is a most eligible and convenient stopping-place for travelers. The guests ever find in its courteous proprietors, Galleher, Nelson & Co., gentlemen who are ever ready to contribute to their comfort and enjoyment.

GALT HOUSE.—South-west corner of Sixth and Main.

METROPOLITAN HOTEL.—On the west side of Main Street, below Second.

HENRIE HOUSE.—North side of Third, between Main and Sycamore.

The visitor to Cincinnati is not favorably impressed during the approach to the city. The railroads entering the city by the valley of Millcreek afford passengers some idea of the extent and situation of the city, but the entrance by river, or by the railroads skirting its banks, conveys an unfortunate idea. The abruptly rising hills crowd all improvements close down to the river side, and almost hide the main portion of the city, till, close at hand, the massive fronts rear themselves suddenly into view. The general aspect is that of solidity, comfort, and commercial prosperity. Wide, well-paved, clean streets, crossing each other at right angles, invite a further inspection. The substantial, elegant architecture of the mercantile and public buildings has illustration in the engravings presented in this volume.

Once comfortably established in his quarters at the

hotel, the visitor is at leisure to make his plans, whether in the way of business or pleasure. A subsequent part of this book will furnish the names and locations of the institutions of the city—civil, benevolent, educational, etc. Directions to excursionists will here be given only in a general way.

The pages immediately succeeding will furnish an idea of the characteristics of different quarters of the city, and a carriage drive of three or four hours will suffice to visit them. Descriptions are also given of the public buildings and works that are worthy of particular attention.

It would be too much for one day, however, to do justice to the various institutions of Cincinnati, in visiting them upon a tour of inspection. A day may be most delightfully spent in a tour among the suburban attractions of the city, including that unrivaled of American cemeteries, Spring Grove. Many visitors also make this city the point of departure upon excursions to the Mammoth Cave and Yellow Springs.

In the city itself, Fourth Street is the center of attraction. There are few more brilliant scenes than it presents upon bright afternoons in the spring or fall, when it is thronged with promenaders, and glittering with the gay and costly equipages of wealth.

Looking down from Fourth Street, one may behold upon the terrace below, convenient to the river, and yet secure from its invasion, the movements belonging to vast manufactures and commerce. He will remember that a territory nearly three times as large as Great Britain draws thence its principal supplies. Some of that immense variety of merchandise will find a destination, by rail or steamer, thousands of miles away— perchance reaching the shores of the Old World. Extending between Main Street and Broadway is a splendid levee, one thousand feet long, with an area of ten acres, lined with capacious steamboats. This, with its narrower extensions up and down the river, is the scene of remarkable activity. "A traveler must, indeed, be difficult to please who can not find a boat bound to a place he would like to visit. From far back in the coal-mines of the Youghiogheny to high up the Red River —from St. Paul to New Orleans and all intermediate ports—one has but to pay his money, and take his choice of the towns upon sixteen thousand miles of navigable waters."

There is a striking view from the levee of the new wire-suspension bridge, which, as James Parton writes, springs out from the summit of the broad, steep levee to a lofty tower (two hundred feet high) near the water's edge, and then, at one leap, clears the whole river, and lands upon another tower upon the Covington side. From tower to tower is one thousand and fifty-seven feet; the entire length of the bridge is two thousand two hundred and fifty-two feet, and it is hung one hundred feet above low-water mark by two cables of wire. Seen from below, and at a little distance, it looks like gossamer-work, and as though the wind could blow it away, and waft its filmy fragments out of sight; but the tread of a drove of elephants would not bend or jar it. The Rock of Gibraltar does not feel firmer under foot than this spider-web of a bridge, over which endless trains of vehicles and pedestrians pass one another. It is estimated that, besides its own weight of six hundred tons, it would bear a burden of sixteen thousand tons. This remarkable work, constructed at a cost of nearly two million dollars, was begun twelve years ago, and has taxed the patience and faith of its projectors severely; but, now that it is finished, Cincinnatians justly look upon it with great pride. One taking the street cars upon Front Street, at the northern terminus of this bridge, may in an hour's ride pass over two suspension bridges, each flung across a navigable river, and will have been, during his ride, in two States, three counties, and three cities.

The great staples of this market—iron, cotton, sugar, tobacco, etc.—are handled along Front, Water, and Second Streets, and their adjacencies. Pearl Street, north of Second, and parallel with it, is the center of operations for an immense capital employed in distributing dry goods, notions, clothing, shoes, etc.

STROBRIDGE & CO. LITH. CINCINNATI, O.

On Third Street are assembled most of the banks,
insurance offices, agencies, lawyers' offices, etc. It is
the Wall Street of Cincinnati.

Fourth Street displays to the visitor the magnificent
retail establishments, and is the fashionable promenade
of the city.

On Third Street, between Broadway and Lawrence
Streets, the stranger may place himself on the former
site of Fort Washington; all traces of which, however,
have long since vanished. It was built in 1789, when
the infant city was hourly in danger of incursion from
the savages who roamed the interminable forests of the
Miami country. The following description is taken
from "Cist's Cincinnati in 1841:" "About the 1st of
June, 1789, Major Doughty arrived with one hundred
and forty men from Fort Harmar, on the Muskingum,
and built four block-houses nearly opposite the mouth
of Licking. When these were finished, within a lot of
fifteen acres reserved by the United States, and immediately on the line of Third Street, between Broadway
and Lawrence, he commenced the construction of Fort
Washington. This building, of a square form, was
simply a fortification of logs hewed and squared, each
side about one hundred and eighty feet in length,
formed into barracks two stories high. It was connected at the corners by high pickets with bastions or
block-houses, also of hewed logs, and projecting about

ten feet in front of each side of the fort, so that the cannon placed within them could be brought to rake the walls. Extending along the whole front of the fort was a fine esplanade, about eighty feet wide, and inclosed with a handsome paling on the brow of the bank, the descent from which to the lower bottom was sloping about thirty feet. The exterior of the fort was whitewashed, and, at a short distance, presented a handsome and imposing appearance. On the eastern side were the officers' gardens, freely cultivated and ornamented, with handsome summer-houses. The site of this building is that part of Third Street opposite the Bazaar, and extending an average breadth of about sixty feet beyond the line of the street on both sides. It was completed by November, and on the 29th of the succeeding month General Harmar arrived with three hundred men and took possession of it."

Many of the dwellings of Cincinnati are remarkable for their handsome proportions and elegance of finish. The east end of Fourth Street, and contiguous portions of Broadway and Pike Streets, exhibit some palatial residences. An object of interest will be the mansion and spacious grounds once occupied by Nicholas Longworth, who was at the time of his death, several years ago, the richest man in Cincinnati. This beautiful estate is now occupied by F. E. Suire, Esq.

Fourth Street, west of Central Avenue, also contains

many handsome dwellings. Prominent amoug them is the residence of Judge D. K. Este.

The West End, comprising a large district lying to the west of Central Avenue, includes the larger number of handsome and comfortable dwellings, and is rapidly growing in extent, beauty, and population.

The district between the Miami Canal, on the south and west, and the hills on the north, contains a population of almost entirely German descent or birth, the number of which is estimated at eighty thousand. This district is known as " Over the Rhine," the Miami Canal receiving this sobriquet. Residents of the city during the Know-Nothing excitement of 1854, well remember the sluggish stream as marking the boundary beyond which it was dangerous for some obnoxious native Americans to venture among the excited foreigners, who are now, as they have ever been, a most valuable element of the population.

Millcreek is at present the western boundary of the city. Plans are maturing to subdue this stream and bring into service a large additional territory which at present is subject to annual inundations. Many acres, which now, every year, at a certain season, are turned into a vast lake by the backwater of the Ohio, will then be covered with valuable improvements, and extend the densely-built city to the base of the western hills.

Upon reaching the heights north of the city, the

scene presented to the eye is one of extraordinary beauty. Three hundred and fifty feet above the river, the position commands a view of portions of two States, three cities, numerous villages, the graceful curve of the river, and the grand sweep of hills. Cincinnati, Covington, and Newport—the two latter divided by the Licking River—and the United States military post on its eastern bank, lie off to the south. On the east may be seen the bold front of Mt. Adams, with its observatory, founded by the distinguished astronomer and noble patriot, O. M. Mitchel, and the beautiful suburb of Walnut Hills; on the west, the magnificent range of hills and the great river winding onward in its ceaseless course toward the Father of Waters. The beautiful suburb of Clifton, with its magnificent country seats, is also visible. Away to the north the eye sweeps over the beautiful highlands, with their splendid mansions and inviting drives, and takes in a portion of the peaceful valley holding in its embrace that most beautiful of cemeteries, Spring Grove. In a clear atmosphere, the charming village of Glendale, twelve miles distant, may be seen. The eye falls also upon the range of hills which bristled with fortifications during the civil war, when Cincinnati was almost a "border city." In 1862, when the city was menaced with attack by a strong army pushing up through Kentucky, every hilltop had its breastworks and heavy cannon, while the

approaches south of Covington were held by a force
numbering at one time not far from twenty-five thousand men.

Across the river, before the present magnificent suspension bridge was completed, stretched a pontoon bridge,
over which many regiments of troops and endless trains
of artillery, wagons, and munitions of war, thundered
over into the "Dark and Bloody Ground," then most
true to its ancient name.

Martial law was first declared in Cincinnati, September 5th, 1862. The ten days ensuing will be forever
memorable in the annals of the city. In an article,
entitled the "Siege of Cincinnati," T. Buchanan Read
wrote thus vividly of them:

"The cheerful alacrity with which the people rose
en masse to swell the ranks and crowd into the trench-
es was a sight worth seeing, and, once seen, could not
readily be forgotten. Here were the representatives of
all nations and classes. The sturdy German, the lithe
and gay-hearted Irishman, went, shoulder to shoulder,
in defense of their adopted country. The man of money,
the man of law, the merchant, the artist, and the artisan,
swelled the lines hastening to the scene of action, armed
either with musket, pick, or spade. Added to these was
Dickson's long, dusky brigade of colored men, cheerfully wending their way to labor on the fortifications.
But the pleasantest and most picturesque sight of those

remarkable days was the almost endless stream of sturdy men who rushed to the rescue from the rural districts of the State. These were known as the Squirrel Hunters. They came in files, numbering thousands upon thousands, in all kinds of costumes, and armed with all kinds of fire-arms, but chiefly the deadly rifle, which they knew so well how to use. Old men, young men, middle-aged men, and often mere boys, dropped all their peculiar avocations, and with their leathern pouches full of bullets, and their ox-horns full of powder, poured into the city by every highway and byway in such numbers that it seemed as if the whole State of Ohio were peopled only with hunters, and that the spirit of Daniel Boone stood upon the hills opposite the city beckoning them into Kentucky.

"The pontoon bridge, which had been completed between sundown and sundown, groaned day and night with the perpetual stream of life all setting southward. In three days, there were ten miles of intrenchments lining the hills, making a semicircle from the river above the city to the banks of the river below, and they were thickly manned from end to end.

"The river also afforded protection by its flotilla of gunboats improvised from the swarm of steamers which lay at the wharves. A storm of shot and shell, such as they had not dreamed of, would have played upon the advancing columns of an enemy, while the infantry, pouring down from the fortifications, would have fallen upon the rear.

"The commanding general congratulated the citizens upon the rally and the result: 'Paris may have seen something like it in her revolutionary days, but the cities of America never did. Be proud that you have given them an example so splendid.'" The Queen City never surrendered.

The beauty of the surrounding hills, which exhibit the gentle and varying slopes peculiar to a limestone formation, is of wide celebrity. There would seem to be no end of eligible building sites in every direction, from which may be commanded most lovely prospects. Many of the mornings in the late summer, when, beneath the rays of the sun, the fog from the river fills all the valley below, afford, from any of the adjacent summits, a view of surpassing beauty. The spectator beholds stretching away from his feet an unbroken expanse, presenting the appearance of a placid lake. Gradually, as the sun ascends the sky, the dense vapors are elevated to rarer regions, and there are disclosed to view the city, the river, the villages, the numerous steamboats, and all the busy life of the valley. More enchanting are the moonlight scenes, when the valley below is wrapped in a mantle of mist, and the beholder may people the weird and shadowy stillness with all the fantastic creations of the imagination.

3

But not the least among the chief attractions of Cincinnati will be its suburbs. These are described at length in a volume soon to be published, a reference to which will amply repay the reader. The vicinity of no city on the continent can furnish more enjoyable drives, more splendid landscape views, or more beautiful residences. The Prince of Wales' party, in 1860, pronounced the suburbs of Cincinnati the finest they had ever seen. All the different suburban localities will amply repay a visit, but no visitor to Cincinnati should fail to see Clifton, Mount Auburn, and East Walnut Hills. Travelers from all parts of America and Europe have declared the prospects from various points in these localities unequaled in beauty anywhere. Particularly may this be said in the autumn, when the Western forests are in their glorious array of color. Here may also be seen the homes of wealth and taste, where nature and art seem to have vied with each other in the production of palatial abodes which might excite the envy of royalty itself. A whole day is not too much to spend in visiting the suburbs, but four hours will suffice to make a shorter circuit, taking in the points already named.

Of great prominence among the objects of interest which Cincinnati offers to the stranger is SPRING GROVE CEMETERY. In natural beauty, it is the finest in the world.

This cemetery is situated in the valley of the Mah-ket-e-wa (the Indian name of Millcreek), three miles north of the present limits of Cincinnati. It is approached by an avenue one hundred feet wide, which is a most beautiful drive. The grounds were selected in 1844, and now contain, with later additions, four hundred and forty-three acres. The numerous springs and groves of noble forest trees suggested the name. The first Board of Directors consisted of the following gentlemen: Robert Buchanan, William Neff, A. H. Ernst, David Loring, Nathaniel Wright, Griffin Taylor, Charles Stetson, J. C. Culbertson, R. G. Mitchell.

The entrance buildings are in the Norman Gothic style of architecture, and cost over fifty thousand dollars. The undulating surface of the ground displays, to the best advantage, the abundant water and forest scenery. Avenues, twenty feet in width, conform to its picturesque character. On every hand are visible evidences of the excellent care of the Superintendent, A. STRAUCH. The entire absence of fences around lots gives the whole the harmony and pleasantness of a park. The monuments are remarkable for their variety and good taste.

The Soldiers' Monument, at the junction of Lake Shore and Central Avenues, was erected in 1864. It is a bronze statue, on a granite pedestal, representing a United States soldier standing on guard. The design was furnished by the sculptor, Randolph Rogers, and the work was cast by Frederick Von Müller, at Munich.

The Dexter mausoleum is the largest and most elegant structure at the present time. It represents a Gothic chapel, and was executed under the care of James K. Wilson, Esq., of Cincinnati.

The Burnet mausoleum is also a costly work of most beautiful design.

There are tasteful chapels which will attract attention, among which are those belonging to the following names: Strader, Selves, Bodman, Worthington, Wiggins, Gaylord, Taylor, Hall, Haynes, and Brown. Marble, Aberdeen and Quincy granite, and brown stone, have been chiefly used for monumental purposes. The monuments belonging to the families mentioned below are notable for beauty of design and finish. They are those of Baum, Carlisle, Clearwater, Davenport, Davidson, Emery, Ernst, Gano, Hale, Hoffner, Holenshade, Hosea, Harkness, Hulbert, Lawler, Longworth, Lytle, L'Hommedieu, Neff, Pendleton, Potter, Patterson, Ringgold, Resor, Shillito, Spencer, Walker, Whetstone, Wilshire, and Williams.

At Carthage, six miles from the city, are the Hamilton County Fair-grounds. Here, in September of each year, the annual county fair is held.

The Trotting Park, at which, in the spring and fall, are held the races, is about five miles from the city.

It may be reached either by railway or by conveyance.

Cincinnati can offer drives of unsurpassed beauty to its visitors. Of those on Spring Grove Avenue, down the river road, across the bridge and out toward Latonia Springs, south of Covington—and last, but not least, out over Mount Auburn, on "the Fifth Avenue of Cincinnati," and through Clifton—the half can not be told. They must be seen to be appreciated.

A grand avenue has been suggested that will completely encircle the city, and afford a drive which will be really magnificent. The plan is to start at a point on the western bank of Millcreek, near the Warsaw pike; thence skirting the base of the hills due north to the Badgeley Run road; thence sweeping around Spring Grove through the thickly-wooded lands of Judge Este; thence on a line due east across the entire rear of the city to the Montgomery road; thence further east to a point which would admit of a southern sweep into and through Pendleton and Columbia to the Xenia pike and into the city, thus completing the contemplated circle.

This avenue would intersect the Badgeley Run road, Hamilton road, Spring Grove Avenue, the Winton road, Carthage pike, Reading road, and Montgomery road, thus affording a drive of five, ten, or twenty miles, as inclination might prompt. Most of the drives which be in the midst, as it were, of a continuous park, so beautiful is the forest along parts of the line.

There will now be given descriptions of the principal buildings and points of interest.

CINCINNATI HOSPITAL.

This imposing structure cost nearly a million dollars, and was opened to the public in January, 1869. It stands upon a large block of ground north of Twelfth Street, between Central Avenue and Plum Street.

The structure, in point of beauty, solidity, and convenience, has not an equal in the country. It stands in a sort of hollow block or square, in the center of which has been placed a large fountain, which, during the hot days of summer, gently throws up many streams of fresh, cool water, moistening the atmosphere and refreshing the shrubs and flowers. This ground will be ornamented with shade trees, shrubbery, and flowers. The main entrance is on Twelfth Street, about midway between Central Avenue and Plum Street. The dimensions of this central part are as follows: seventy-five feet wide by fifty feet deep, supporting a main entrance, with a spacious hall directly through the middle. Upon the first floor of this block the Superintendent and family have their apartments; and appropriate apartments, such as an apothecary room and dispensary, pathological museum, reception rooms, and a library

CINCINNATI HOSPITAL.

for the resident physician, are arranged. The basement has convenient rooms for storage purposes, and for the examination of drugs. There is also a laboratory, laundry, and drying chamber, bathing rooms, cellars, and other places of a similar character.

The second story is devoted to the accommodation of officers for sleeping rooms, and a few private wards are on this floor for patients who wish to have extra care, and are able to pay for it.

The third story contains a large room that is intended for the operating lecture room, with seats for the accommodation of some seven hundred and fifty students. In addition to this lecture room, there are apartments expressly adapted for patients both before and after operation, rooms for operators and their instruments, lavatory and bath room.

The structure is of brick, with freestone finishings. A Mansard roof, in slate of variegated colors, extends the entire length. One section is surmounted by a dome and spire one hundred and ten feet high. The accompanying engraving will present an excellent view. No more complete or extensive building of its kind exists anywhere. The grounds are 448 by 340 feet.

CINCINNATI COLLEGE EDIFICE.

This edifice, on Walnut Street, between Fourth and Fifth, is one hundred and forty feet front by one hundred deep, and is built of white limestone, in the Doric style. It is occupied in part by the Chamber of Commerce, the Young Men's Mercantile Library, and the Law School of Cincinnati. The hall of the Chamber of Commerce is one hundred and thirty-six by fifty feet. This building belongs to the endowment of the Cincinnati College, and the income annually accruing from it is swelling a fund, which, at no distant day, will contribute to erect a grand free university.

THE FACULTY OF THE LAW SCHOOL

are Bellamy Storer, LL. D., Professor of Legal Rights, including Real Estate, the Domestic Relations, and Pleadings and Practice; George Hoadly, Professor of Equity Jurisprudence; J. D. Cox, Professor of Commercial Law and Evidence.

THE COUNTY COURT-HOUSE,

on Main Street, north of Ninth, is a massive structure, built of Dayton stone, costing at the time of its erection, before the era of high prices, $500,000. Immediately in the rear of it is the County Jail, with which there is subterranean connection.

The opposite engraving of this magnificent edifice will give a better idea of it to the reader than any

description. Here is transacted the multitudinous business pertaining to the civil administration of Hamilton County.

Here is the Law Library of the Cincinnati Bar, which is practically one of the best law libraries in the country, having been selected by practitioners with a view to the actual demands of practice. It contains the American, English, Irish, Canadian, and Nova Scotian Reports, and a large collection of American and English Statutes, besides the standard text-books.

THE OHIO MECHANICS INSTITUTE

is a substantial structure, on the corner of Sixth and Vine. It contains at present the rooms of the Public Library, and also is the temporary home of the Theological and Religious Library.

The Tower of the Fire Department is on this building. Its lofty summit commands a bird's-eye view of the whole city. From its deep-toned bell the midnight alarm of fire wakes the city with its dreadful note.

CHURCH EDIFICES.

Among the more costly and elegant church edifices, may be mentioned Trinity Methodist Episcopal, on Ninth Street, west of Race; St. John's Episcopal, corner of Plum and Seventh; First Presbyterian, on Fourth Street, near Main, with a steeple two hundred and seventy feet high; Central Presbyterian, corner of Mound and Barr Streets; St. Xavier's Catholic, on Sycamore Street, near Seventh; and the Ninth Street Baptist, east of Race Street. The latter is considered to have the most tasteful audience room in the city. The congregation of Morris Chapel (Methodist) are engaged in the erection of an edifice which will, when completed, be the finest in Cincinnati. Their location is on the corner of Seventh and Smith Streets.

There are one hundred and nineteen churches in Cincinnati, divided as follows among the various denominations: Baptists, eleven; Christian, one; Congregational, four; Disciples of Christ, four; Friends, two; German Evangelical Union, four; German Reformed, three; Independent Methodist, one; Jewish Synagogues, five; Lutherans, three; Methodist Episcopal, sixteen; Methodist Episcopal, German, three; Methodist Protestant, three; Methodist Calvinistic, one; Methodist, colored, one; New Jerusalem, one; Presbyterians, Old School, six; Presbyterians, New School, six; Presbyterians, United, three; Presbyterians, Reformed, three; Protestant Episcopal, seven; Roman Catholic, twenty-three; United Brethren in Christ, three; Universalist, one; Unitarian, three, Union Bethel, one.

CITY HALL.

S. W. Cor. Fourth & Race.

THE CITY HALL,

with the beautiful grounds in front, occupies the square west of Plum Street, lying between Eighth and Ninth Streets. This is an attractive part of the city. The accompanying engraving will place it distinctly before the eye. It was built in 1853. All the city officers are here to be found. The sessions of the School Board, the City Council, and the Police Court attract to this edifice a multitude of people, whose conditions widely differ. Thus "the extremes" of humanity meet.

THE CINCINNATI OBSERVATORY

is situated near the eastern limits of the city, on Mount Adams, five hundred feet above low water, and has a commanding view of the city, the river, and the surrounding hills. It is furnished with a most perfect equatorial telescope, whose focal length is seventeen and one-half feet, with an object-glass twelve inches in diameter, which has magnifying powers ranging from one to fourteen hundred times. The corner-stone of this edifice was laid by the statesman and scholar, John Quincy Adams, in 1843, and the institution is inseparably associated with the memory of the astronomer and patriot, General O. M. Mitchel.

THE CINCINNATI ORPHAN ASYLUM, THE HOUSE OF REFUGE, THE WIDOWS' HOME, AND HOME FOR THE FRIENDLESS

are fully described in their respective places in the chapter upon the charities of Cincinnati.

THE CUSTOM-HOUSE BUILDING,

a view of which is given, is an ornament to the city. It is on the south-west corner of Fourth and Vine Streets, and is the property of the United States. Here are the depository of government funds, the post-office, United States courts, and other offices pertaining to the general government.

THE CARLISLE HOUSE,

on the corner of Mound and Sixth Streets, is a handsome structure. A hotel, upon the European plan, is here conducted in the best style. The apartments are spacious, and constructed purposely with a view to their present use. Few private dwellings excel this house in the tastefulness and elegance of its internal appointments.

CITY WORK-HOUSE.

In 1866, a tract of twenty-six acres, near the House of Refuge, was purchased by the city, and in the succeeding year work was commenced upon this magnificent structure. It will be, when completed, the finest

POST OFFICE.

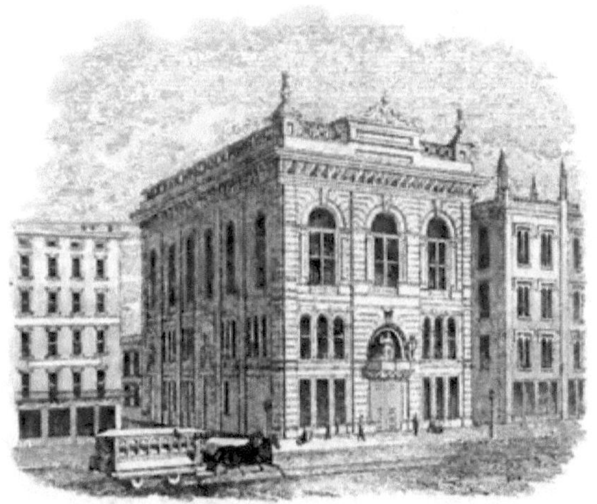

MOZART HALL.

WORK-HOUSE.

building of the kind in the United States. The edifice is five hundred and ten feet long, and will contain six hundred apartments. The work-shops will form a hollow square in the rear of the structure. The total cost will be nearly three-quarters of a million dollars. The accompanying engraving will give an idea of the edifice. The work will reflect great credit upon Robt. Allison, Esq., the Chairman of the Building Committee, and Messrs. Anderson & Hannaford, the architects.

THE DAVIDSON FOUNTAIN.

This magnificent work of art is soon to be erected upon Fifth Street, between Walnut and Vine. It receives its name from its munificent projector, Tyler Davidson, who was long one of the merchant princes of Cincinnati. The execution and details of the project, at the death of Mr. Davidson, were left in the hands of Henry Probasco, Esq. The conditions imposed upon the city in the gift were, briefly : That the fountain should always be kept in good order, with an abundance of pure water, and free for the use of all; that the conduits should be kept supplied twelve hours of the day in summer, ten hours a day in the spring and fall, and six hours a day in winter, except when the mercury was below a freezing point; that a competent person, detailed from the police, should always be kept near it to preserve its cleanliness, and to guard it from abuse; that the water should be used only for drinking and ornamental purposes, except in case of fire, in the immediate vicinity, and that to the donor and his legal representatives should be reserved the right to hold the city responsible for the continued fulfillment of these conditions.

The design of the fountain is beautiful, and it will stand an enduring monument to the liberality and taste of Messrs. Davidson and Probasco. The principal figure will represent the Genius of Water, from whose hands falls the ever-flowing rain, which is caught by a peasant standing on the right, whose fields are thirsting for it. On the opposite side stands a citizen imploring water for his burning house. On the opposite side is the figure of a man, who, by a vigorous stroke, opens a spring for one on crutches who desires to drink. On the other side is a mother leading her child to the bath, invited by a nymph playing with the springing jets of water. Four jets, two from above and two from below, add life and variety to the scene. Near the base are four *bas reliefs*, representing the utility of water, viz., navigation, mills, fisheries, and steam.

On four corners are figures of children suggesting the enjoyments connected with water, viz., a girl adorning herself with pearls, a boy fishing for shells, a second fitting on skates, and a third finding corals

and crystals. Near the top **of the** fountain, or **just**
under the main figure, will be placed a medallion **of**
Tyler Davidson. The water coming from the **leaves**
of the shell is **to** be used **as a fresh drinking water by**
a separate conduit pipe. **The four upper** jets belong
only to the decoration, and are not intended for practical use. The whole fountain will be **of bronze,** the
base and its surroundings of granite and **porphyry, and**
the railings or protection of the **foundation will be either**
of wrought-iron or Dayton **stone.**

The entire height of the structure from the street **to**
the crown of the topmost figure **(itself seven feet)** will
be thirty-two feet and **a half.**

The entire cost **of the fountain will not** fall **far short**
of $100,000. When completed **it** will be the finest af-
fair of the kind in **the** United States, and **not inferior
to any in Europe.**

THE GARDEN OF EDEN.

The avenues have **been** surveyed, and **a force em-**
ployed to grade the same. **The work** has since been
steadily prosecuted, and the avenues now graded wind
along the hill-side, **surrounding the** reservoir, **until,**
almost imperceptibly, **you are** brought to the highest
elevation, **where** numerous points present themselves,
from which magnificent views of the lake-like reservoir
can be seen, as well **as a grand** and majestic view of

the Ohio River, with the picturesque hills of Kentucky in the distance.

The whole tract now controlled by the city embraces one hundred and sixty acres. The intention is ultimately to convert it into a great city park, in which shall be a new and capacious reservoir. For this it is admirably adapted. The grounds are all within the city limits, and, when opened, can be reached in fifteen minutes from the corner of Fourth and Vine.

It may be remarked that no sites hitherto spoken of compare with this in point of eligibility and susceptibility of improvement. The great advantages of the Garden of Eden can be realized only by those who visit and explore it.

The views from some of the avenues can not be surpassed in point of grandeur and sublime effect. Nature has left very little to be done by the landscape gardener. The center of the ground is so undulating and diversified that ample scope will be found by the landscape engineer to add to the natural interest by here and there constructing an artificial bridge where the windings of the path make it necessary to cross some deep gully or murmuring stream; by the erection of grottoes and artificial rock-work, and other devices calculated to please the visitor. Several fine lakes can be made, with little expense, by making earth-work dams across one or more ravines, arranging them at different elevations, thus making the lake at the highest point supply those below it. Beautiful cascades will be thus formed, presenting charming views from the avenues along either bank. And these lakes, so graceful and beautiful in the summer, will be no less beautiful in the winter, when their icy surfaces shall ring with the steel-clad shoes of the skaters.

The work on the new reservoir was commenced in 1867, and already sewers have been constructed, and the greater portion of the underground work and foundations has been done.

ACROSS THE RHINE.

The manufacture of lager beer employs an immense capital in this city. Its consumption is annually on the increase. The product in Cincinnati amounts to many millions of gallons annually.

Lager beer can be made to advantage only in the winter season. It is indispensable that it have ample time to ripen in the cellar before use. There are many immense cellars, in some of which five hundred thousand gallons of beer can be stowed away. One phase of German life, and one not uninteresting, can be seen only in the gardens where lager beer is dispensed in the summer season. Many of them are thronged during the warm evenings.

GYMNASIUM BUILDING.

Prominent among the many handsome fronts on Fourth Street is that occupied by the Gymnasium. This association was organized in 1853, and a successful career encouraged it to attempt the splendid improvements here referred to, which were entered March 12, 1869.

THE EXERCISING ROOM.—This magnificent hall is about one hundred and twenty feet in length, forty-five feet wide, and thirty feet high, making one of the most spacious apartments for the purpose which could have been selected. Lining the walls, are some two hundred and twenty-five closets, neatly constructed, for the safe keeping of the apparel of the members during their exercises. At the further end of the hall are dressing-rooms, where the street attire may be changed for the more convenient habit of the gymnast. The arrangements of the apparatus in this vast room are all that can be desired for bringing into action and fully developing every muscle of the body. For evening exercises this hall is lighted from the ceiling by a system of suspended reflectors of immense size, which throw a mellow and softened light over the whole room, avoiding shadows, which side-lights sometimes cause. This experiment has resulted in a grand success, not only removing one of the chief causes of accidents, and effecting a pleasing illumination, but attaining, withal, an economy in the consumption of gas, which is of no minor importance. The appointments in other particulars are in keeping with those already mentioned. The beautiful marble drinking fountain, and the wash-room, finished in the highest style of the plumber's art, are noteworthy.

READING ROOM.—After the fatigue of an hour in the exercising room, there is a charming retreat for a quiet few moments in glancing over the papers and periodicals, of which there is an abundant supply, suited to all tastes; or, if reading be irksome, chess and checkers are at hand, and may be indulged in. The reading room is finished in green. The carpet is a beautiful Brussels, is of excellent quality, and in its selection exhibits again that marked taste which the Committee has shown throughout. The furniture is handsome, and about the whole there is an attractive and comfortable appearance.

BATH ROOM.—The bath room is about fifty-five feet long by seventeen wide, and contains a large number of closets. The baths are of iron, and of the most approved pattern. These, as well as the platforms, are raised to prevent the accumulation of dirt, and to secure an easy access to any part in scrubbing. The painting is most beautiful and tasteful, the colors blending harmoniously. The most happy effect is arrived at. The toilet, the mirrors, and various accommodations are of the most excellent kind. Warm and cold water is supplied, with showers, etc. The heating apparatus is a conical furnace, capable of heating a large boiler, containing some fifty barrels of water, in twenty minutes. In every respect, this important department is perfect.

The Young Men's Gymnastic Association numbers now over twelve hundred members, which will undoubtedly be largely increased. The officers are: A. P. C. Bonte, President; J. B. Resor, Vice-President; L. Norton, Secretary; William Resor, Jr., Treasurer. The Directors are Howard Barney and A. W. Whelpley.

HUGHES HIGH SCHOOL.

This is an imposing edifice, in the collegiate Gothic style of architecture. It is on the south side of Fifth Street, facing Mound Street, whose southern termination is immediately opposite. The octagon towers at the corner give the building a striking and novel effect. No expense was spared to make it one of the most perfect of its kind. The internal arrangements are admirably adapted to the requisites of a school of the highest order.

LANE SEMINARY,

at Walnut Hills, is described in a subsequent part of this volume.

WOODWARD HIGH SCHOOL,

on Franklin Street, between Sycamore and Broadway, is an institution well worth visiting. Under the care of Professor George W. Harper, who has been for some years the Principal, this school has not only retained, but enhanced its ancient reputation.

THE JEWISH TEMPLE,

on the corner of Plum and Eighth Streets, is a point of great interest to visitors. Its style of architecture is peculiar and costly, and its internal appointments splendid in detail. The building, as is the case with all similar structures, faces to the west, in conformity to Hebrew custom. Religious services are held here every Saturday morning, at 10 o'clock.

KEPPLER'S.

This edifice, owned by Keppler & Brother, is one of the finest in Cincinnati. It is an elegant freestone front thirty-eight by one hundred and thirty feet. Their elegant saloon, elaborately furnished, is one of the chief attractions of the city. Here a substantial meal, or lighter refreshments, can be obtained, served up in the best style. Special efforts are made to provide for the entertainment of ladies. A visit to this will repay any one. It is one of the fashionable resorts.

LINCOLN PARK,

on the west side of Freeman, near Clark, is a beautiful pleasure ground. It is handsomely laid out, and needs only time to develop into a spot of remarkable attractions.

THE CITY PARK

is on Plum Street north of Eighth.

HOPKINS PARK

is on the corner of Mt. Auburn Avenue and Saunders Street.

WASHINGTON PARK,

on the north side of Twelfth, between Race and Elm, is the oldest of the public pleasure grounds. It was formerly the Presbyterian burying-ground of the city. Its noble trees, beautiful lawns, fountain, and other beauties, are much enjoyed by the multitudes who frequent it.

LONGVIEW ASYLUM FOR THE INSANE

is situated near Carthage, about six miles from the city. It is a magnificent structure, and attracts the notice of every passenger upon the railways entering the city by the Millcreek valley. The imposing front of this edifice and its extent strike the attention of all. The internal arrangements are admirable, and all its

LONGVIEW ASYLUM.

appointments constitute it one of the most perfect institutions of the kind in the country. Dr. O. M. Langdon is the efficient Superintendent and Resident Physician, and visitors receive at his hands the utmost courtesy and attention.

This is a State institution, and is controlled by a Board of Commissioners appointed by the Governor of the State.

The edifice is built of brick, and is six hundred and twelve feet long. It is almost fire-proof. The stairways are of iron, and the floors are laid in cement. There is an abundant supply of water, and numerous independent means of egress in all parts of the house, thus lessening the danger of loss of life in case of fire. The upper stories of the wings are devoted mostly to convalescents, and contain the amusement and reading rooms, which are well furnished. The building is lighted by gas manufactured on the premises, and is heated partly by hot air and partly by steam. There are over six hundred apartments in the Asylum. It was completed in 1860, and cost, in the low prices of that period, nearly half a million of dollars.

Its architect was Isaiah Rogers. Extensive pleasure grounds are well cared for, with a view to the exercise and recreation of inmates. In 1868, 149 patients were admitted—79 males, 70 females. The average number, 430. Expenses for the year, $110,501.21.

LONGWORTH'S WINE CELLAR.

Of this Mr. Parton says : "One of the established lions of the city; it cheers the thirsty soul of man. There we had the pleasure of seeing, by a candle's flickering light, two hundred thousand bottles of wine, and of walking along subterranean streets lined with huge tuns, each of them large enough to house a married Diogenes, or to drown a dozen Dukes of Clarence, and some of them containing five thousand gallons of the still unvexed Catawba. It was there that we made the acquaintance of the 'Golden Wedding' champagne, an acquaintance which, we trust, will ripen into an enduring friendship. If there is any better wine than this attainable in the present state of existence, it ought, in consideration of human weakness, to be all poured into the briny deep."

MARINE HOSPITAL.

This is a substantial, solidly-built edifice, one hundred feet square, on the corner of Lock and Sixth Streets. The building is thoroughly fire-proof, and has every facility for the comfort and welfare of its inmates. Ample verandas extend along the front and sides.

THE MASONIC TEMPLE,

on the north-east corner of Third and Walnut, deserves special attention. It is in the Byzantine style of architecture, and fronts one hundred and ninety-five feet on Third Street by one hundred on Walnut. It is one of the most magnificent edifices of its kind in the United States.

In the third story are a Chapter Room, Royal Select council room, Banquet Hall, twenty-one by fifty-eight feet, a Knights Templar's Encampment asylum, and many other apartments. A part of the fourth story is devoted to a Grand Lodge room, forty-three by seventy feet.

MOZART HALL,

on the corner of Vine and Longworth Streets, is a massive stone building, with an auditorium that will seat three thousand persons.

THE OHIO MEDICAL COLLEGE,

on Sixth Street, west of Vine, is admirably adapted to the uses for which it was built. It contains two large lecture halls, with extensive apartments for museums, dissection rooms, etc.

PIKE'S OPERA-HOUSE,

on Fourth Street, between Vine and Walnut, is a magnificent structure. The original opera-house was totally destroyed by fire, in March, 1866. The present edifice reproduces the front of the first building, but the internal arrangement is completely changed. It contains one of the most beautiful music halls in the United States. The front is of fine sandstone, wrought in the architectural style of the Elizabethan age, with elaborate emblems of the fine arts cut in relief. This block, with the adjoining buildings, extending from Walnut Street to Vine, makes one of the most imposing displays of architecture to be seen in any American city.

THE PASSENGER DEPOTS

of the Atlantic & Great Western, the Cincinnati, Hamilton, & Dayton, and the Indianapolis, Cincinnati, & Lafayette Railways are model specimens of architecture. The first is between Fifth and Sixth Streets, on Hoadly Street. The last mentioned is entered on Plum Street, below Third.

QUEEN CITY SKATING RINK,

on Freeman Street, between Laurel and Betts, is a lively place in the winter; and at all seasons is a point of attraction for amusement seekers.

THE UNION SKATING POND

is west of Lincoln Park, and is the scene of hilarious gayety when Jack Frost is abroad in earnest. In the milder seasons this is the chief point of interest for the devotees of base ball.

ST. PAUL'S METHODIST EPISCOPAL CHURCH.

This edifice, which is now in process of erection upon the corner of Seventh and Smith Streets, will be an ornament to the city. The audience room, with the galleries, will accommodate fifteen hundred persons.

ST. XAVIER'S COLLEGE,

on the corner of Sycamore and Seventh Streets, is one of the noticeable buildings of Cincinnati. It fronts sixty-six feet on Sycamore Street, and one hundred and sixty-six feet on Seventh Street. The institution was established in 1828, and about ten years afterward it passed into the control of the Society of Jesus, under the auspices of which the present structure was erected. Over the entrance is carved the motto, "*Ad majorem Dei Gloriam.*" The impression conveyed by this edifice is that of massive grandeur and strength, and a durability measured only by time itself.

ST. PETER'S CATHEDRAL.

Among church edifices, the most imposing is St. Peter's (Roman Catholic) Cathedral, which is one of the finest buildings in the West. It is built of white limestone, with a stone spire of remarkable symmetry and beauty, two hundred and fifty feet high, resting on a colonnade of Corinthian columns. It was completed in 1853, about eleven years after its commencement. Here are to be witnessed all the imposing ceremonials of the Catholic ritual service. The music of the choir and splendid organ attracts many visitors.

RAILROAD BRIDGE.

The projected bridge across the Ohio, between But-ler Street, in this city, and Saratoga Street, in Newport, will be completed in 1870. It will furnish transit for railway trains, vehicles, and foot passengers.

The structure will be of wrought iron, timber being used only in the flooring. There will be eight piers and seven spans.

The following are the officers of the Newport and Cincinnati Bridge Company: President, Alfred Gaither; Vice-President, A. S. Berry; Secretary, Charles H. Kilgour.

Directors: M. J. King, Wm. Ringo, W. H. Clement, T. G. Gaylord.

SUSPENSION BRIDGE.

This grand achievement of engineering skill is else-where described. Its execution was due to the genius of John A. Roebling, Esq. Its entire cost was about two million dollars. The entire length is nearly half a mile. The span is the longest in the world. The

STROBRIDGE

NAT'L O.

rate of toll for foot passengers is three cents; for a horse and carriage, fifteen cents.

SCIENCE AND BACON.

The visitor to Cincinnati in the winter season will be interested in the various processes of pork-packing. It is quite a sight to witness the rapid disposition of the huge animal at the hands of skilled workmen. The following description is given of the process after the slaughtered hog is delivered on the cutting-table: "Two simultaneous blows with a cleaver sever his head and his hind-quarters from the trunk, and the subdivision of these is accomplished by three or four masterly cuts with the same instrument. Near the table are the open mouths of as many large wooden pipes as there are kinds of pieces in a hog; and these lead to the various apartments below, where the several pieces are to be further dealt with. Away they start on their journey, and thus in twenty seconds the six hundred pounder has been cut to pieces and duly distributed." The pork business of Cincinnati is enormous, and is the source of great wealth.

TOUR TO THE MAMMOTH CAVE.

A brief allusion to the Mammoth Cave may not be out of place here. No tourist to the West should fail of visiting this wonder of the world. It is situated in Edmondson County, Kentucky, ninety miles south of Louisville.   A stage ride of ten miles from Cave City, which is nine hours' ride from Cincinnati, on the Louisville and Nashville Railroad, brings one to the Mammoth Cave. It is within half a mile of Green River. The cave is dry and exceedingly conducive to health. The most timid need not fear to enter it. It is visited by many invalids for the purpose of inhaling its air. The uniform temperature in the cave the year round is 59°. It has been explored ten miles in an advancing line, and probably over fifty miles, including the lateral branches of its avenues.

So bracing is the air and exciting the novelty of the trip, that even ladies accomplish the eighteen miles without fatigue.

No description can do justice to the beauty and grandeur of this most wonderful cavern of the globe, with its avenues, domes, cataracts, rivers, immense chambers, and beautiful calcareous formations.

WATER WORKS,

on East Front Street, near Little Miami Depot. Few persons who have not visited these works have a correct idea of their magnitude. The capacity of the present reservoir is five millions of gallons. The quantity required for the city daily is about eight millions. Thus, it will be seen that the supply has to be replenished

nearly twice each day. To furnish this the ponderous engine is but leisurely at work, its pumping capacity being eighteen millions of gallons each twenty-four hours. A clearer idea of the immense power of this machinery may be obtained by reflecting that, at each revolution, it lifts two thousand gallons of water, making, at present speed, six thousand gallons per minute, while it has the capacity of lifting sixteen thousand gallons.

CINCINNATI WESLEYAN FEMALE COLLEGE.

From "The Ladies' Repository" are taken the following items relative to this noble institution. It is located on Wesley Avenue, between Court and Clark Streets:

The foundations of the College were laid in the summer of 1867, and on the 26th of September an immense congregation assembled on the grounds to witness the laying of the corner-stone, and the dedication of the new grounds and uprising buildings.

No description could give a better idea of the elegant, commodious, and durable structure than is given by the engraving. Its internal arrangements and finish are in keeping with its external appearance, and in its adaptations to all the purposes of a female college, both for the residence and for the instruction of the pupils it would be difficult to conceive any thing more perfect. It is claimed that the Wesleyan Female College, of

Cincinnati, was the first institution in the land, for females, bearing the high privileges conferred by a college charter.   Among its founders were Bishop Morris, L. L. Hamline, Charles Elliott, J. L. Grover, G. C. Crum, W. H. Lawder, Adam Miller, William Nast, T. Harrison, L. Swormstedt, J. P. Kilbreth, and William Herr. They were wisely directed in the selection of a first President.   Rev. Perlee B. Wilber was chosen, and for seventeen years, with the assistance of his estimable and efficient wife, most energetically and successfully conducted the educational interests of the institution. But few teachers succeed in so thoroughly impressing themselves upon the minds and hearts of their pupils as did Mr. Wilber. His name is yet fragrant among the Alumnæ, and his power and influence are yet felt in the destinies of the institution.

In 1859, Mr. Wilber died, and was succeeded by Rev. Robert Allyn, D. D.   He was followed by Rev. R. S. Rust, D. D., who for three years energetically, and with increasing patronage and prosperity, conducted the institution till it became necessary to retire from the old college buildings, and to suspend the school till the erection of the new college.

YELLOW SPRINGS

may deserve a mention here. It is seventy-four miles north-east of Cincinnati, and is thus easily accessible by

rail. Here is located **Antioch College, which is in**timately associated with **the memory of** Horace Mann.
Adjoining the college **plat, on the east, is a highly**
romantic and picturesque **ravine, affording all the scenic**
variety of **overhanging cliffs, waterfalls, isolated rocks,**
and numerous gushing **springs, deeply** embowered, and
climbing vines, and clustering **evergreens, threaded with**
varied walks, and inviting to their **cooling shade.** Yellow Spring is about **half a mile north-east of the col**lege. **It discharges from a crevice in a limestone rock**
over **one hundred gallons of water per minute.**

In the neighborhood **is an** enchanting **spot called**
Clifton, which affords **some of the most beautiful scen**ery in the West. **Here the Little Miami River, in the**
course **of a few miles, falls two hundred feet. These**
falls have **cut a narrow channel, to a great depth,**
through solid rocks **of limestone. The banks are cov**ered with **hemlock, cedar, and other evergreens.**

There are **excellent hotels at Yellow Springs, and, in**
the summer season, no place **in the country is more**
worthy of a visit. **The** Neff **House is well known.**

PALACES OF TRADE.

A tour among the notable places of the city will comprise the magnificent **retail stores of Cincinnati. These**
are, with some exceptions, **on Fourth Street, west of**
Main. Shillito's, **Hopkins', DeLand's, Boutillier's,**

5

Lewis & Livingston's, and Wilson's establishments will display a profusion of fabrics which are the peculiar delight of womankind. The rich treasures of art will meet the eye at Bonte's and Wiswell's, where can always be seen productions of Cincinnati artists, who have a national reputation. At McGrew's, Duhme's, Smith's, and Owen's, are ranged in all their tempting beauty and costly array, the fascinations of the jeweler's art.

Leininger & Buhr, and the St. Nicholas, are ever ready to cater to the appetite of the hungry tourist.

The principal carriage stand is on Vine Street, south of Fourth. The banks of the city open at nine o'clock and close at three. At the end of this volume will be found the routes of horse-cars and other information of use to the stranger.

CHAPTER IV.

CINCINNATI AND ITS FUTURE; ITS GROWTH, INDUSTRY, COMMERCE, AND EDUCATION.

ATURE has given Cincinnati a situation which is at once beautiful and attractive. If one should in imagination go back eighty years, and stand on the site of old Fort Washington, he would see the Ohio flowing gently through an amphitheater surrounded by hills. This amphitheater is a broad, expanded plain, which the Ohio enters on the north-east and passes out on the south-west. This natural plain is about twelve miles in circumference, and is almost exactly bisected by the river. Looking up from this plain, the hills seemed to bound the horizon on every side; but they are only apparently hills—hills really to the plain below, from which they rise rather abruptly, but, in fact, only on the level with the great interior plain which descends from the lakes of the North to the Valley of the Ohio. This great interior plain is cut through by the river; and this is a great advantage to Cincinnati, for on every side there are interior valleys which make the outlets of its internal line of commerce. Opposite is the mouth of the Licking; on the sides are the two Miamis; on the south of the present city is Millcreek; through a ravine at the north runs Deer Creek; and thus the circling hills were pierced by nature, as if for the very purpose of opening out those lines of commerce which were to make the arteries of a great inland city, and which, as they interlocked to the north, made numerous summits and vales—the future sites of palaces and gardens. Looking from the plain at the surrounding hills, they present none of the gloomy or rugged aspects of Alpine grandeur; on the contrary, they are soft, and beautiful, and picturesque. Nature presented neither the sublime nor the monotonous, but formed the gentle and diversified hills to represent the temperate clime, the genial soil, and the well-watered land of this bright and fruitful region. At the time we spoke of, the flag of Fort Washington was floating gracefully in the western breeze, but all around were the native forests. An old Indian chief said that he had often looked down from the eastern hill (where the Observatory now is) to see what the white people were doing in the fort. Soon the red man cast his last look upon the Ohio; the fort, the Indian, and the forest disappeared together; civilization came with its burning force, destroying the natural face of creation, but instituting new features and elements, growing by the vigor of new forces, and presenting new forms of beauty.

We shall not trace the history of Cincinnati, but proceed to inquire what right it had to be a great city—what its growth has been—and what prospects it has in the future. *Why* did Cincinnati grow so rapidly? what are its elements of growth? and why should it not grow with renewed vigor? These questions involve an analysis of what the city is, and what it may be—an analysis which may be useful to both the citizen and the coming immigrant.

1. The first element in the success of Cincinnati which is permanent, and, without a revolution in nature, must forever continue, is its *position*. Perhaps no city was ever more fortunate in this particular. Cincinnati is central to the Ohio Valley. From the junction of the Monongahela with the Alleghany (which is the real Ohio) to the Mississippi is nine hundred and sixty miles. From Lake Erie to the sources of the Kanawha and the Tennessee (in Virginia and North Carolina) is five hundred miles. The average breadth of the valley is three hundred miles. Taking from this a strip on the lakes, and the district immediately round Pittsburgh and Wheeling, and there is remaining a country of two hundred thousand square miles in surface watered by the Ohio and its great tributaries, and fruitful with every product, of which Cincinnati is the geographical center, and to which all its products and resources must tend. It is thus by nature made a great central mart of trade

and industry. Situated one thousand five hundred miles from the ocean, it is yet connected by navigable waters, not only with the ocean, but with that immense interior river coast, which runs interlacing the whole country from the Rocky Mountains to the Alleghanies. Vast as is this great region, if it had been like the steppes of Asia or the plains of Africa, Cincinnati might yet have failed of greatness, but the Valley of the Ohio is the very garden of nature. There is no need of recounting its resources; for every traveler who descends the Ohio sees in the smiling vales and forest-crowned hills the evidences of great natural wealth. Nor need we recite how, in the bosom of the hills and under the sandstones of the valley, there lie those inexhaustible beds of mineral riches which may employ the industry of men through future ages. The geologist describes them, the miner digs them, and the cunning artificer in the work-shops of Cincinnati employs them in all the forms and purposes which civilized man demands.

We may answer now the question, What right had Cincinnati to be a great city? It was like the right of man to use his faculties. God gave to this position and these resources not only the right, but the necessity of creating a city which must be one of great magnitude and power. It is true, this city might have been a few miles above or below its present site, but even that is doubtful; for it was attempted to found the city at both Columbia and North Bend, but the attempts failed; and the city seems to have been built here almost by a decree of Providence. At any rate, so far, Providence has favored both the sagacity and the industry which have here raised up the Queen of the West.

Such were the advantages of Cincinnati by its natural position and resources, and we shall now see how it grew, and what is its present magnitude and strength. Here the first element is its *growth in population.* However great the riches of nature, it is Man which brings them out and makes them useful. To Man, then, we must look as the artificer of cities. The growth of Cincinnati was for many years extraordinary, but in the last ten years has been slower. The same temporary lull in activity and growth has happened to all cities at the same period in city life. It happened to New York and to Philadelphia, and, of itself, means nothing, but the very obvious fact that in cities, as in men, the vigor of youth can not always be kept up at the same rate. But the great question is, whether, like New York and other great cities of the world, its vigor shall revive after this period, and its growth be continued in proportion to the extent and resources of the magnificent country of which it is the center? That question we shall consider; but, first, we must see what its growth has been, and what it is.

The growth of population may be shown in two simple tables—one its actual growth, and the other its growth compared with other cities:

In 1810, ...	2,320	
In 1820, ...	9,602	
In 1826, ...	16,230	
In 1830, ...	24,831	
In 1840, ...	46,382	Increase, 85 per cent.
In 1850, ...	115,436	" 150 "
In 1860, ...	161,044	" 39.51 "
In 1869, ...	230,000	" 43 "

In the last line is included the northern suburb, which is now as much a part of the city as any ward in it. The population, by the census of 1870, will probably show an increase of forty-five per cent., and be an increase in the preceding ratio.

The following table will show the increase of New York and Philadelphia at the *same period of their growth*, beginning with one hundred thousand inhabitants; thus:

NEW YORK.		PHILADELPHIA.	
In 1820, ... 123,706		In 1820, ... 137,097	
In 1830, ... 202,581		In 1830, ... 188,961	
In 1840, ... 312,710		In 1840, ... 258,037	

It will be seen that from 1820 to 1830, New York increased sixty-three per cent., and from 1830 to 1840, but fifty-four per cent—but little more than the ratio of increase in Cincinnati since 1850. Philadelphia increased, from 1820 to 1830, thirty-nine per cent., and from 1830 to 1840, but thirty-seven per cent. Thus, Philadelphia increased, at the same period of its growth, less than Cincinnati has in the last twenty years; yet New York has one million of inhabitants, and Philadelphia has seven hundred thousand. This fact proves that great cities grow, not by sudden and temporary causes, but by the continual development of their natural resources.

The original elements of population in Cincinnati were chiefly from New Jersey and Pennsylvania, a people remarkable for thrift and industry. A few families of Germans came out, and settled at an early period, and were among the best class of citizens. But the German immigration did not come in very strongly till 1830; but from that time till 1860, the German current has set toward this city with great force. The proportion of this element to the whole population may be seen in the following table taken from the census:

Citizens of German birth in 1830,				. . . .	5 per cent.
"	"	"	"	" 1840,	. . . .	28 " "
"	"	"	"	" 1850,	. . . .	27 " "
"	"	"	"	" 1860,	. . . .	30 " "

It will be seen that the German citizens continue in nearly the same proportion, a little more than one-fourth the whole number. In 1860, there were one hundred and sixty-one thousand and forty-four persons within

the city limits, and it may be curious to see in what
manner, as to nationalities, they were composed. The
proportions were as follows:

Americans, ... 87,430,	54 per cent.	
Germans, ... 48,931,	30 " "	
Ireland, ... 19,375,	12 " "	
All other foreigners, . . . 5,308,	4 " "	

Now, in 1869, the proportion of nationalities has not
materially changed. The Germans are still next to the
Americans in number and weight. Of native Americans, three-fourths are natives of Ohio, showing that
the native population is rapidly rising up, and the period
is not remote when the population of Ohio will be nearly
homogeneous. The children of Germans and Irish are
born here, and soon outnumber the natives of Europe.
It may be remarked, that *one-fourth* the whole foreign
born population of Ohio is in Cincinnati; showing that
relatively much the larger proportion of foreign born
people go into the towns. The reason of this is, that
the rural population of Europe emigrate much less
than the artisans and laborers, and the latter seek the
towns for employment. The effect of this upon Cincinnati has been decided and favorable. The German
population contains many mechanics and artisans whose
skill and industry increase the thrift and wealth of the
city. This brings us to another element of society, the
OCCUPATION of people. The census of 1860, showed

that there were in Cincinnati **THREE HUNDRED AND FORTY** (340) different *occupations*. Of these, *two hundred and thirty* were mechanic's, artisans, and manufacturers. This simple fact speaks volumes for the industry of the city, and shows the real foundation of its prosperity. Almost every conceivable human art is carried on here; and this is a conclusive evidence of the great advantage to artisans and manufacturers, settling in Cincinnati. For it is a settled principle, proved by much experience, that it is a great help for all kinds of artisans to be where there is a great variety of arts carried on, because there are all the material and workmen which are necessary to aid and carry on every branch of arts or manufactures. Beyond doubt, this has been one reason why so many workmen and mechanics of all kinds have actually come to Cincinnati for the last twenty years.

In this respect there has been both cause and effect, for an examination of the *occupations* in Cincinnati for the period between 1850 and 1860, shows that in ten years there was an actual increase of *fifty* kinds of occupations which did not exist before. In 1860, there were twenty more occupations in Cincinnati than in Chicago, and fifty more than in the State of Indiana. The tendency of these facts is to make Cincinnati the great central market and distributor for the whole Valley of Ohio, and to make it what Paris is remarkable for, the great emporium of all kinds of arts needed, used, and dis-

tributed through a great empire. The United States is
now of imperial dimensions; but what the United States
now is, the Ohio Valley alone will be in a few years.

Having now glanced at the number, composition, and
occupations of the people of Cincinnati, let us look
at the products of their industry. In that must at
last be found the sources of wealth and prosperity.
A city does not feed itself. It must go outside of itself
to find bread, and therefore must have something to
exchange for it, and what is above this constitutes its
increasing wealth. What it exchanges for food must
necessarily be the products of its industry. While the
commissions on merchandise imported may be large
and profitable, making many engaged in commercial
business wealthy, the great body of the people can pros-
per only by the results of industry. This is true even
of the City of New York, the most commercial city in
the country. We have seen that Cincinnati is remarkable for the variety of its occupations and arts; let us
see what they have produced.

2. The second element of Cincinnati is its *industry;*
and the progress of industry, represented in money
values, may be thus expressed:

<pre>
In 1840, value of products, ... $17,432,670
In 1850,   "   "   50,000,000
In 1860,   "   "   56,000,000
In 1869, estimated, ...   60,000,000
</pre>

These results are, no doubt, very imperfect, because all canvasses of the manufacturing elements of the country are imperfect, from the want of a proper skill and discrimination in taking them. But the above totals are sufficiently near for the purpose of comparison. If it be asked why there was so moderate an advance in the last few years on the production of 1850, it may be answered, that four or five years of war, by draining off able-bodied men, actually diminished the products of manufactures; and it may be added, that for three or four years prior to the war, the continual agitation and ill-feeling had diminished the demand in the South-west for the products of Cincinnati. These causes have all ceased, and a new era is opening for the industry of this city.

The main branches of productive industry in Cincinnati are very nearly as follows:

Iron, of all kinds,	$5,500,000
Furniture, of all kinds,	1,700,000
Meats, of all kinds,	9,000,000
Clothing, of all kinds,	4,500,000
Liquors, of all kinds,	4,500,000
Soap and Candles,	1,500,000
Oils, Lards, Resins, etc.,	3,000,000
Mills, of all sorts,	2,000,000

These are only approximations, but are sufficiently near to show what are the great branches of manufacturing industry in Cincinnati. The export of these products is mainly to the South and West, and, it is quite obvious, must increase in proportion as population is increased in those directions. The pacification of the country, the restoration of confidence, and the rapid extension of population, are all in favor of the manufacturing industry of Cincinnati. In the year 1860, the relative industry of the Western cities was as follows, taking the counties in which they lie as the proper rule of comparison :

Alleghany County (Pittsburgh),	. . .	$26,563,379
Cook County (Chicago),	. . . .	13,555,671
St. Louis County (St. Louis),	. . . . .	27,610,070
Jefferson County (Louisville),	. . . .	14,135,517
Hamilton County (Cincinnati),	. . . .	46,995,062

It will be seen that, nine years ago, the products of industry in Cincinnati were several million dollars in value greater than those of Chicago and St. Louis put together, and greater than those of St. Louis and Louisville put together. No doubt, these proportions have considerably changed since 1860, Chicago having grown greatly, and Louisville being prosperous; but it is plain that, as a manufacturing place, Cincinnati is much superior to any other Western city. It is also superior in manufactures to any city of the United States, except New York and Philadelphia. Perhaps no fact can better prove the great advantage of Cincinnati for artisans and laborers; for, unless this large class of citizens felt themselves well off and prosperous, no such advance in industry by so young a town could possibly be made; and unless there were extensive and profitable markets for the products, the manufacturers could not sustain themselves. But here, in this center of the Ohio Valley, there is cheap food, abundant material, and markets for the products, extending through the immense region from Central Ohio to Northern Alabama, and from the Alleghanies to the Rocky Mountains. It is not strange, therefore, that so many kinds of arts and manufactures should have risen up here, nor that they will continue to extend till this great and fertile region shall be filled with people, and its towns glow with the industry of untold millions.

3. With industry comes COMMERCE. Commerce is the creation of labor, for there must be something to exchange before any thing can be got. A city, however, filled with arts and manufactures need not be confined to its own productions. On the contrary, what the country produces must come to the city for a market, and the country must there buy what it needs. The city, therefore, in addition to the actual production of its citizens and workmen, is also the exchange for the commerce of both producers and consumers. Cincinnati is the great exchange for the whole Ohio Valley, and has grown as largely in commerce as it has in

industry. The annual reports of the Chamber of Commerce, compiled with great care, show this fact in vivid colors. The value of the principal articles of imports and exports for the period from 1854 to 1864, were:

	Imports.	Exports.	Total.
In 1855, value of	$67,095,741	$88,777,394	$105,873,135
In 1860, " "	103,347,216	77,037,188	180,384,406
In 1864, " "	389,790,537	239,079,825	628,860,362

The average value of gold in 1863–'4 was 55 premium; so that the aggregate value of imports and exports in that year when reduced to gold was $314,430,-181. The *proportional* value of 1855, 1860, and 1864, were represented, respectively, as 105, 180, and 314. Thus, in ten years the aggregate commerce of Cincinnati has increased 200 per cent. This may have been exceeded in ratio by new and small towns, but no large city in the country increased at a greater rate in the same period of time. This rate of increase was three times that of population in the same period; and hence, as we shall presently see, an equal growth in the wealth and resources of the city. It proves, in fact, that the citizens of Cincinnati had in that time been prosperous, and increased largely in capital and in the profits of trade, as well as in numbers. From 1860 to 1865, the war actually reduced the commerce of Cincinnati in many things; but, on the other hand, a great deal of new business sprung up to supply this deficiency. The trade in tobacco increased tenfold; that in coal, salt, leather, and wood doubled; in boots and shoes trebled, while the general trade in dry goods increased also. These facts prove, that so great were the resources of Cincinnati in the productive country around it, that even the depressing effects of the war on a border city— from which commerce on one side was nearly cut off— could not arrest its progress. In the whole loyal country no town was as liable to damage, commercially, as Cincinnati. It was damaged by the war, but has since recovered rapidly, and its commerce has expanded with a natural and healthy vigor. If we inquire in what directions the trade of this city extends, we shall not be restricted to the mere commerce of the Ohio and the Mississippi, whose interior coasts extend tens of thousands of miles, but we find even its small products passing over half the globe to reach the remote nations of Europe and of Asia. Its crackers have been exported to China and its candies to Greece. It is on the Atlantic coast where most of its vast exports of breadstuffs and provisions may be found. Its largest export trade has been with New Orleans, Memphis, and other Southern ports, whence its products are distributed through the entire South. By the way of Baltimore it finds access to the coasts of Virginia and the Carolinas, where the hams and the flour of the Miami Valley are consumed by thousands, with whom Cincinnati has.

6

as yet, no railroad connection. This fact is suggestive of what may be done hereafter to extend the direct commerce of Cincinnati to the whole Southern coast.

The manufactured articles of Cincinnati go chiefly to the West and South-west; in other words, to the new settlements, where furniture, stoves, candles, and articles necessary to the comfort of a household are chiefly needed. Among these articles is the *home* itself; for one of the curiosities of Cincinnati is the making and exportation of houses by wholesale for the new farms and towns of the great valley. Far down the Mississippi, over the plains of Kansas, and on the waters of the Missouri, the Cincinnati manufacturer has put up whole houses, every joint and floor of which have been sawed, planed, and grooved in Cincinnati. In the same regions, the mills, the plows, the machinery necessary to carry on agricultural life have been made in this city. Resources of industry and commerce like these can not be limited by competition, or exhausted in growth till, in some future age, the country shall be like China, filled with its hundreds of millions of people.

4. If industry creates commerce, so commerce must be carried on by LINES OF INTERCOMMUNICATION with all parts of the country. Cincinnati was early to see the need of these. It is now forty years since the Miami Canal was made. At that time canals were all

the rage, and Ohio made more than four hundred miles of canal, and the benefits expected from them have been fully realized. Cities, towns, villages, and cultivation have sprung up in their course, and even now, with all the prodigious competition of railroads, the canals carry an immense amount of produce and merchandise. The Miami Canal, which was then only intended to reach Dayton, has since been extended to Toledo, and connects with the whole lake region.

Soon after the completion of the canals, the farmers became intent on turnpikes ; for no sooner was a great and easy artery to the city made, than the necessity of turnpikes to communicate with it became evident. Cincinnati engaged heartily in it, and there is now no district of country better supplied with good roads than is the Miami Valley. The twelve counties composing the Valley have now one thousand five hundred miles of turnpike and plank roads, all of which tend directly or indirectly to this city. These, with the common farm roads, make more than six thousand miles of roads, by which the farm produce of this fertile region is carried off to its great markets.

More than thirty years ago, when the Baltimore Railroad had been completed to Frederick, the subject of railroads was agitated in Cincinnati, and promptly was the work begun. The Little Miami Railroad was the first made, but was soon followed by the Hamilton and

Dayton, by the Indianapolis, by the Covington, and by
the Ohio and Mississippi, till now there is no city—and
we speak advisedly—which has more or more extended
railroad communications than Cincinnati. It is cus-
tomary with Chicago, St. Louis, and Philadelphia to
speak of their railroad lines which enter the city as
theirs, although they may extend across half the continent. In one sense this is correct, for if a railroad
enter Cincinnati from the East, and another from the
West, and both connect with other lines over the continent, bringing freight and passengers from town to
town, those lines may fairly be said to belong to that
city as much as to any other. A line which connects
Cincinnati with Chicago belongs as much to one as it
does to the other; and a line which goes directly to the
Atlantic cities belongs as much to this city as to New
York and Philadelphia. If this were the rule of cal-
culation, Cincinnati, being entirely central, would have
the advantage over either. But to give a correct and
proper view of the railroad system of Cincinnati, we
will give two tables of railroad distance, one bound by
State lines, and the other of direct continuous lines
centering here, and terminating in other large cities.
The city of Cincinnati is central to three States—Ohio,
Indiana, and Kentucky. There is no large city in either
of them to compete with it except Louisville, which is not
half its size, and competes but little with its commerce.

This being the case, we may very properly take the railroads of these States as being centralized at Cincinnati and connected rather with it than with any other place. The following table presents the number and the length of railroads in these three States, viz.:

	NO.	MILES.
Ohio,	36,	3,500
Indiana,	14,	2,500
Kentucky,	5,	700
Railroads,	55,	6,700

Here are over six thousand miles of railroad in the three States, whose central city is Cincinnati. The two States of Ohio and Indiana have a mile of railroad to every fourteen square miles of surface, an amount which is not equaled on any equal surface in the United States. When we consider the newness of the country, and the small amount of active capital compared with older States and countries, this is an extraordinary result, and sufficient to show that Cincinnati has now internal communications enough to drain every pound of surplus products in the region tributary to herself on the north side of the Ohio. But when we look south of the Ohio, we see comparatively a blank. The whole State of Kentucky has only about seven hundred miles of railroad, of which only two hundred are really tributary to Cincinnati. In the one hundred thousand square miles of territory south of the Ohio, whose whole trade must hereafter come to this city, extending to the mountains of North Carolina, there are only five hundred miles of railroad, four-fifths of which does not touch Cincinnati. This is a region, too, rich in all the resources of nature, and it is perfectly certain that these resources must soon be developed by the energy of enterprise and the power of capital. For half a century the idea, rather than the reality, of slavery (which existed only to a small extent) prevented men and capital from going where that shadow continued to rest. But now it is gone, and nothing can prevent that flow of people and energy which heretofore went only West, but will now pass the Ohio, and develop the rich regions of the South.

In order, however, to look at the railroad connections of Cincinnati in another point of view, yet which connects it with other cities, we give a table of direct lines to them:

	LINES.	MILES.
To Baltimore,	2	840
To Philadelphia,	1	668
To New York,	2	1705
To Toledo,	1	202
To Chicago,	2	650
To St. Louis,	2	717
To Louisville,	1	105
To Lexington,	1	100
	12	4,987

There are five thousand miles of railroad on the DI-
RECT LINES to the principal cities, and which, with
their lateral branches, will make an aggregate of at
least seven thousand miles. To Baltimore the routes
are by Wheeling and Parkersburg; to New York, by
the Central and the Erie; to St. Louis, by Vincennes
and by Terre Haute. The direct railroad lines to each
of these cities are respectively:

	MILES.
To Baltimore,	506
To Philadelphia,	668
To New York,	764
To Chicago,	294
To St. Louis,	340
To Louisville,	105

It will be seen that the shortest line of railroad to
tidewater is to Baltimore; but the distance to Norfolk
and Charleston, on the Atlantic, is no more than to
Baltimore, while that city is one hundred and fifty
miles from the ocean. It is apparent, therefore, that if
a direct Southern line is made to either Norfolk or
Charleston, it will command the Atlantic freight from
Cincinnati to Europe.

The summary of the facts above presented, in regard
to the commercial intercommunication of Cincinnati,
exhibits some extraordinary results in the narrow
Valley of the Miami, all of which is tributary to Cincinnati. There are:

	MILES.
Canals,	100
Turnpikes,	**1,600**
Common Roads,	4,500
Railroads,	500

In the three States tributary to this city, there are six thousand seven hundred miles of railroad, and in the *direct* lines centering in the city there are five thousand miles. We have not the means of comparing this exhibit with the best districts of Europe, but it exceeds any thing to be found in an equal space of this country. Chicago is probably the nearest; but the three States of Illinois, Iowa, and Wisconsin have not yet exceeded Ohio, Indiana, and Kentucky in railroads. All New England and New York do not exceed, in miles of railroad, the three States which lie around Cincinnati. But we need not proceed with these comparisons. It is evident that the broad plains and fertile vales, the inexhaustible beds of iron and coal, and the now fast-accumulating capital of cities and towns, will cause and compel, in all time to come, the largest amount of intercommunication which can belong to any great commercial center.

5. Where industry, commerce, fertile lands, and numerous lines of communication exist together, individual PROPERTY and AGGREGATE WEALTH must grow and accumulate. Let us, for a moment, see how Cincinnati stands in regard to wealth. The assessed values

of property are never accurate, and always below the true values; but these assessments serve very well for a comparison, and to show the growth of capital **by the gradual** accumulations of industry and commerce. The following table shows the valuations **of** property **in** Hamilton County (in which Cincinnati is) for a series of years:

Value of all property in 1841,	. . . . . . $10,760,494
Value of all property in 1850,	. . . . . . **55,670,631**
Value of all property in 1860,	 119,508,170
Value of all property in 1869,	 166,945,497

These statements are taken from the Annual Report of the Auditor of State, and are sufficiently accurate to show the progress of the city **in** wealth and capital. From 1850 to 1869, the **value of** property increased threefold, and, in the past nine years, thirty-two per cent. The main increase is in money, merchandise, banks, and manufactures. These have, in nine years, increased nearly forty millions of dollars. This proves that Cincinnati is now passing through the same change, in the kind and growth of its wealth, which New York and Philadelphia passed through at the same period of their growth. In the first period of building up **a** considerable city, all the accumulations of capital go into real estate and manufactures, so that there is a deficiency of commercial capital; but, after this, when **cities become** self-sustaining, commercial and banking capital is increased, and the valuations form a much larger proportion of money, merchandise, and stocks. This period, New York passed through thirty years ago, and Cincinnati is going through now. With the increase of capital, comes also more frequent sales of property, more loans, and more building. This may be seen in two lines, exhibiting the deeds made, the money loaned on property, and the new buildings in the years 1859 and 1867—the one before the war, and the other since, and showing the change in eight years:

	1859.	1867.
Deeds, ...	4,560	6,697
Money on Mortgages, . .	$6,642,225	$12,739,512
New Buildings, ...	683	1,372

Perhaps nothing can show the true condition and progress of Cincinnati better than this table. It shows that, just previous to the war, the progress of this city had been much checked, but that, since, its former growth has recommenced. There is now more building and more sales of real property than has been known for many years.

6. With new buildings and new growth, there comes the need of PUBLIC IMPROVEMENTS, and, accordingly, the public mind, which has only recently thought of Cincinnati as something more than a mere inland town, has been quickened and excited with the idea of public works which may adorn and improve the true

metropolis of the West. It is but a short time since was completed, by an incorporated company, the most magnificent suspension bridge in the world. When the bridge at Niagara was built, it was considered one of those extraordinary things which could hardly be equaled; but the Cincinnati bridge surpasses that. It spans the entire River Ohio, and, at the height of one hundred feet in the air, admits the passage of the largest steamboats. Another bridge over the Licking unites Newport and Covington; so that now the Queen City and her Kentucky daughters sit in a united, compact, and graceful circle on the waters of the Ohio, and in the splendid amphitheater which nature has provided for them.

The bridging of the Ohio, being thus commenced, is not to end with this. It is now certain that every great arterial line of railroad passing from the great lakes of the North to the Southern sea-board must, to be successful, cross the Ohio on bridges; accordingly, the Baltimore and Ohio Road is building one at Parkersburg; and so, also, the great roads which connect New York and Philadelphia with Cincinnati seek to bridge the river, that they may connect fully with the line now, or hereafter to be, made from this city to the South. The bridge from Newport to this city, which is understood to be in the interest of the Pennsylvania Railroad, is begun, and will progress to completion. The roads terminating in the west of the city have a charter, and anticipate building a bridge below. Thus, it takes no great imagination to see that cities on both sides of the Ohio, united by bridges and streets, will seem to be one harmonious whole.

With the bridges comes also a vision of parks and avenues. The city council have already authorized and laid out three great avenues, corresponding to the natural outlets of the city; and as the city climbs the hills and extends into what were once mere rural shades, these avenues will also ascend the furthest summits, and unite the pleasures of the country with those of the city. The street car, that most convenient of modern inventions, will go with them. But there will still be needed also great breathing places—parks; and parks the people will have, although no great progress is made yet. On the east of the city, near the hill where the old Indian chief looked down on the garrison of Fort Washington, the city has a large piece of ground called Eden Park. There the new water reservoirs are to be placed; and when such a park shall be filled with water, trees, and shrubbery, and one shall look down on this vast city, and follow with the eye the winding Ohio, it can not be said that Cincinnati is without one of the most beautiful walks and gardens which natural beauty or artistic skill has produced for any city. Other parks and other adornments will come with time, and the

charms of nature be enhanced by the improvements of
man.

7. With all this growth of industry, commerce, and
material improvement, Cincinnati has never forgotten
that mind is superior to matter, and that to educate the
people is the highest obligation of a civilized community. Hence, from the very beginning, means have
been taken to promote popular education, till now,
every child in the city can be educated in the most practical branches of knowledge; and, by the sagacity and
liberality of individuals, means have been provided for
the foundations of the highest institutions of learning.
A brief outline of the schools, seminaries, and colleges
of Cincinnati will serve the purpose of this general
description.

At the basis of education in this city are the PUBLIC
SCHOOLS. To these all youth, between the ages of five
and twenty-one, have access. According to the law of proportions, established by the censuses, this comprehends
thirty-nine per cent. of the whole population, and at the
present time gives ninety thousand seven hundred youth
within the legal age entitled to public instruction. Of
these only about twenty-five thousand are in the schools
at any one time; but ten thousand others are in the
parochial and private schools—making in all thirty-five
thousand at one period in course of education. Some
persons have compared this with the whole number

entitled by law to attend the schools, and hence inferred that there must be great numbers of children who do not attend school at all, but this is a great mistake. The children of the poor and working classes, which are the greatest number, are withdrawn from school at not more than twelve or thirteen years of age, and nearly the whole body of youth in school are withdrawn before they are eighteen years; so that the attendance in the schools is by classes and installments, and probably thirty-five thousand is as many as can be expected to be in attendance at the present time. Probably not more than one in a hundred escape instruction at any school, and those who do not attend more than one-third of the time to which they are entitled, nevertheless get what are called the rudiments of knowledge. But some one may ask, How come ten thousand in parochial and private schools? The great body of these are in the Roman Catholic parish schools. They originated in consequence of the dissatisfaction of the Catholics with the conduct of the public schools. Parish schools are attached to nearly all the Roman Catholic churches, and contain several thousand pupils. In addition to these are many private schools and seminaries, especially those for girls, which are preferred by some parents on account of special instruction, particularly in the ornamental branches which they afford.

In 1860, there were forty-six schools and seminaries,

parochial and private, in Cincinnati, of which twenty-seven were Roman Catholic, containing nine thousand and six hundred pupils, but the number is no doubt increased. There are now in this class of schools and seminaries fully twelve thousand. The public schools of Cincinnati have, in recent years, been crowned by the high schools, institutions, which, in their general character, are the same with what are commonly known as "colleges," and in regard to law, may be made to comprehend universal knowledge, for the law does not restrict their studies. Of these one is for boys and the other for girls. Both have been founded by the sagacity and liberality of early pioneers—William Woodward and John Hughes—from whom they are called the Woodward and Hughes Schools. The pupils of these colleges are the graduates of the common schools. At each annual examination a certain number of those who have passed out are entitled to enter the High Schools, and thus they may pursue, so far as they have time and ambition, the highest range of studies. The list of subjects pursued in the high schools, as returned in the annual reports, shows that to these students is open every branch of learning attainable in any of our colleges. Then the public system is perfected by the establishment of a graduated system of instruction, which leads the minds of youths, if they give time to it, from the very alphabet of knowledge to the higher regions of learning. It is to give their children the benefits of these schools that many families have come to Cincinnati, and thus the institution of the public schools has added to the wealth as well as the intelligence of the city.

After the public schools, we may mention the colleges and professional seminaries, some of which were founded long previous to the public schools. The earliest of these is CINCINNATI COLLEGE, with whose name and history is associated the honored memory of the oldest and best founders of the city, originally chartered as a purely literary seminary. It was for many years a regular college, in which many youths were educated. Having ceased its work for a period, it was again revived as a college and a medical school; but has now, for several years, been continued as a law school. In the meantime it has been relieved of all embarrassments by the payment of its debts, and possesses an unincumbered property worth $200,000. It is proposed to make this fund, in connection with some other, the foundation of the future University of Cincinnati.

Within a few years Mr. McMicken has given a large estate for the education of youth in Cincinnati, subject to some limitations, and intended ultimately to found a college or university. The property has been so managed by the trustees as to be at present a large endowment for whatever institution they may hereafter erect.

ST XAVIER COLLEGE, CINCINNATI, O.

We may, therefore, expect that the McMicken University will be a fact of the future.

The ST. XAVIER COLLEGE (Roman Catholic) has been many years in existence, and pursues a regular course of instruction, chiefly conducted by the Jesuits.

In addition to these literary institutions, there are professional schools—law, medical, theological, and commercial. There is but one LAW SCHOOL, which is a branch of Cincinnati College, and has been thirty years in successful operation. In that period it has had several professors distinguished for legal learning, for social standing, and political influence. It has graduated twelve hundred students, among whom may be found men who have adorned the bench and the bar, society and government.

The Medical Schools are the oldest professional institutions, and have always had large numbers of students. The Medical College of Ohio was founded half a century since, and has probably graduated thousands of pupils. The Miami Medical College is a newer institution, but with an able Faculty, and promises much future usefulness.

The Physio-Medical College teaches the peculiar doctrines of what is generally termed the Botanical School.

The College of Dental Surgeons is one of the evidences that, in recent years, dentistry is treated as a science. This is, perhaps, the reason of the established fact that American dentists enjoy the highest reputation in all foreign countries. The College of Dental Surgeons in Cincinnati has added to both the skill and the reputation of the profession.

Of theological schools, there are two—one Roman Catholic, on the summit west of Millcreek; and the other Presbyterian, on Walnut Hills. The latter, Lane Seminary, is well endowed, has considerable income, and maintains a regular course of theological teaching.

Another class of colleges, so called, are the commercial. These, however, do not pretend to teach what is usually understood as a collegiate course, but simply those practical elements necessary to commercial business.

From what we have said, education for the masses, and for the common business of life, is well provided for. Every child may have some sort of education, and every one intended for business may here acquire well the elements of his profession; and for those who wish to be instructed in science and the classics, the High Schools afford an opportunity; yet, for high scholarship, the youth of the city must look to the coming, rather than the present colleges. The Cincinnati College Fund, the McMicken Fund, the Observatory, and some others which may be gathered in, would be sufficient to lay the foundation and build up the stately structure of a future university. Whether they can ever be united and concentrated for such a purpose, we know not; but after contemplating the noble and liberal contributions, private and public, made here for the universal instruction of the people—after seeing so many tens of thousands already brought into the schools, and so many other thousands who have gone forth from these institutions as merchants, lawyers, physicians, and clergymen, to be useful and honored citizens of the republic—after all this, we can not help thinking and hoping that this broad and spacious edifice of popular education may be crowned with a Cincinnati University. Then the work of the children will well compare with that of their fathers, and scholars of profoundest learning go forth from the city which already furnishes the arts, and manufactures, and commerce which adorn and improve the Valley of the Ohio, and hence made herself the Queen of the West.

We have now finished our outline sketch of the growth of this city and of its principal elements. We said nothing of the young cities on the opposite shore, or of the far-extending suburbs to the north; but we may return for a moment to contrast this scene as it was observed by Judge Symmes eighty years ago, with that now seen from Eden Park, and that which will be seen in some future. Then, the proprietors of the Miami country saw with delight this beautiful amphitheater surrounded with its wood-crowned hills; but then the forest was unbroken, solitude rested on the bosom of

Nature, and the Red Indian looked with suspicion on the approaching white man. Now, the forest is cleared away, a great town is built up, silence is fled, the incipient roar of clanging industry thunders upon the ear, the voices of shouting multitudes are heard, and the visitor to Eden Park beholds these cities filling the valley below. The temples of God and the schools of youth, the factories of art and the vessels of navigation rise in the midst of forty thousand houses, filled with three hundred thousand people!

Such is the present scene compared with that when civilized man came to conquer the wilderness of nature. But it is not improper, and it will require no extraordinary gift of prophecy to look a little into what the future may, and probably will, produce. Cincinnati has now reached the period when, as New York did thirty years ago, it is passing from the condition of a respectable town to that of a great city, where, in fact, capital is sufficiently accumulated and public spirit excited to make these extensive improvements, which both vitalize its resources and adorn its aspect. Most of these we have already mentioned in this sketch, but we may group them together: first, the natural resources around the summit hills, the gentle curves of the hills, and their decline to the north, have made the suburbs of Cincinnati the most beautiful in the United States. No other city can compare with them.

Then, to enjoy these suburban scenes, come the avenues: these will wind up the ravines, finally pass north of the hills, meet the valley beyond, and thus make splendid boulevards, to which no others can compare. Then come the parks: these will be on the hills or in the northern valley, and, being reached by street cars, will make lovely and healthy country gardens for the resort of all classes of people. Then the reservoirs on the hills will furnish living fountains for the avenues and the gardens. Far to the west, in the Valley of Millcreek, what has heretofore been a great mud lake will be leveled and filled, built up, and the city extend to the western hills as it does to the eastern. Then the gardens and the avenues will crown the western summits. In the meanwhile, the great railroad bridges over the Ohio will have been built, the Southern railroad will be seen as one of the great arteries of commerce, and the young cities of Newport and Covington will climb the hills of the south, as Cincinnati does those of the north. Then will be seen, on some of the surrounding points to the north, the University, and, near it, the Observatory; and science and letters, and the beautiful arts, will crown the scene which industry, and commerce, and education have created. Then, if a kind Providence shall favor the labors of man, the Cincinnati of the future will be, as it has been, the metropolis of the Great Central West.

CHAPTER V.

City Government—School System—Board of Health—Police and Fire Departments—Administration of Justice.

THE government of municipal affairs in Cincinnati devolves upon a mayor, a city council composed of two members from each ward, and a board of city improvements composed of the mayor, city civil engineer, and three city commissioners.

The city elections occur on the first Monday in April, most of the officers serving for a term of two years.

Candidates for council are required to be freeholders, and residents of the city three years previous to the election.

The following gentlemen occupy at present city offices as respectively named:

Mayor.—John F. Torrence.

CITY COUNCIL.

James W. Fitzgerald........................*President.*

WARD.

    1...T. F. Eckert...............J. W. Fitzgerald.
    2...Wm. Loder...............Chas. Kahn, Jr.
    3...V. Eichenlaub ....Conrad Schultz.

4...Wm. H. Glass............P. F. Maley.
5...Daniel Wolf..............J. S. Hill.
6...B. C. Corbett ....T. Cannon.
7...L. C. Buente ....David Baker.
8...James Morgan............A. P. C. Bonte.
9...Chris. Von Seggern.....Jos. Eveslage.
10...Joseph Siefert............A. Wagner.
11...H. B. Eckelman.........Jos. Kinsey.
12...Jacob Benninger.........G. W. Ziegler.
13...G. A. Doherty ....M. Corbett.
14...Wm. H. Harrison.......R. M. Moore.
15...A. T. Goshorn...........T. F. Baker.
16...Drausin Wulsin ....W. H. Brickell.
17...James B. Doan ....A. K. Brookbank.
18...Clinton Buente..........Samuel Beresford, Jr.
19...F. W. Schwencker......L. C. Frintz.
20...A. E. Jones..............Wm. Kirton.

CITY AUDITOR.—CHAS. H. TITUS.

CITY TREASURER.—ROBERT MOORE.

CITY SOLICITOR.—J. BRYANT WALKER.

CITY CIVIL ENGINEER.—R. C. PHILLIPS.

CITY COMMISSIONERS.—JOHN H. LAWRENCE, L. MC-
HUGH, THEODORE CHAMBERS.

JUDGE OF POLICE COURT.—WALTER F. STRAUB.

CHIEF OF POLICE.—

PROSECUTING ATTORNEY OF POLICE COURT.—MOSES
F. WILSON.

The public school system of Cincinnati has long been celebrated for its efficiency and the liberal scale upon which it is conducted. The efforts of such men as Nathan Guilford, John P. Foote, George Graham, and Samuel Lewis, established a broad foundation for future growth. The details of its workings can not, for want of space, here be given. The Annual Report, which, itself, constitutes each year quite a volume, may be referred to for all necessary information. A Board of Trustees, elected by the people, administer the business affairs. A Board of Examiners, appointed by the City Council, decide upon the qualifications of teachers.

John Hancock is the Superintendent of Schools. His administration has evinced great ability, and the schools have never been more prosperous than at present.

The Board, during 1868, made arrangements to open a Normal School, for the training of females intending to qualify themselves for teaching. The inauguration of this plan marks a new and important era in our system, and success seems to await it.

The following regulations exist for the government of the schools :

"None but the children of actual *bona fide* residents of Cincinnati shall, under *any circumstances*, be admitted to the common schools, *free;* but children of non-residents may be admitted by the Trustees of any district, on payment, in advance, to the Clerk of the Board, the following tuition fees, viz.:

"For admittance into intermediate schools, at the rate of twenty dollars per annum; district schools, sixteen dollars per annum—payable, in each case, semi-quarterly, quarterly, semi-annually, or yearly."

The regular meetings of the Board of Examiners are held at the Office of Public Schools, City Buildings, on Eighth Street, between Plum and Central Avenue, on the second Thursday of each month, except July and August, at two o'clock P. M.

The Board grants two grades of Certificates, denominated, respectively, Male Principal's Certificate and Female Assistant's Certificate.

Candidates for a Male Principal's Certificate are examined in Spelling and Definitions, Reading, English Grammar, Geography, American History, Mental Arithmetic, Written Arithmetic, Algebra, Theory and Practice of Teaching, Natural Philosophy, Constitution of the United States, Ancient and Modern History, Anatomy and Physiology, Chemistry, Astronomy, Geometry, English Literature, and Penmanship.

Candidates for a Female Assistant's Certificate are examined in Spelling and Definitions, Reading, English Grammar, Geography, American History, Mental Arithmetic, Written Arithmetic, English Literature, Theory and Practice of Teaching, Natural Philosophy, Constitution of the United States, Anatomy and Physiology, Penmanship, and Ancient and Modern History.

Candidates for positions in the High Schools will be examined in Chemistry and Astronomy, in addition to the above list.

The number opposite to each branch, in the column on the right of the list of studies on the certificate issued, measures the result of the examination, ten being the maximum. Less than seven, in either English Grammar, Geography, Mental Arithmetic or Written Arithmetic, is a failure. Certificates are valid as follows: For an average of seventy per cent. of correct answers, one year; eighty per cent., three years; ninety per cent., five years.

A record of the character of the examination of each individual is preserved in a volume for the use of the Board of Education.

Candidates who have not taught in the Common Schools of Cincinnati, must leave with the Clerk of the Board, at least three days before the monthly meeting. a certificate of good moral character, together with a declaration that they are eighteen years of age, (or seventeen, if graduates from the High Schools, or with similar attainments), and that they design to teach in the Public Schools of Cincinnati, if found qualified. Candidates are requested to leave their address, and a statement of any experience they may have had in teaching.

Candidates shall be **examined in the absence of all** spectators, save the members **of the Board of Education.**

Candidates shall **not be examined who are not** present, punctually, at the **appointed hour.** None shall be admitted **to a second examination, till after the** expiration of six **months.**

No Certificate shall **be issued without an average of** seventy per cent. **of the full number of marks.**

The Board will **grant no certificate to any candidate** who entirely fails **in any branch of study in which an** examination is **required by the Board.**

Graduates of **the Normal School have preference in** the selection of **teachers for the schools.**

One **week prior to the annual opening of the schools** each year, **all the teachers of the Common** Schools shall be required to attend **a Teacher's Institute, held in the** city. Such institute shall **be open to all persons who** may desire to **become teachers in the Common Schools** of Cincinnati.

The salaries **of teachers in the Cincinnati Schools** range from $400 **per annum to $2,100.**

The following **are the names of the members of the** Board **of Education, for the years 1869–70, commencing** in July:

WARD.

1...J. H. Brunsman......W. J. O'Neil.
2...Peter Gibson...........J. W. B. Kelly.

3...C. C. Campbell.........E. M. Johnson.
4...D. J. Mullaney........Benj. J. Ricking.
5...Dr. Wolfley............H. W. Poor.
6...F. Macke................J. P. Carberry.
7...C. F. Bruckner........H. P. Siebel.
8...C. H. Gould...........J. C. Christin.
9...F. W. Rauch..........Joseph Kramer.
10...Wm. Kuhn.............H. L. Wehmer.
11...S. S. Fisher............
12...A. Themkaupf.........J. C. Krieger.
13...George D. Temple...Wm. McClennan.
14...Henry Mack...........G. W. Gladden.
15...A. D. Mayo.............Abner L. Frazer.
16...Francis Ferry..........John P. Storey.
17...S. A. Miller............J. L. Drake.
18...A. Bohling.............Louis Ballauf.
19...S. F. Wisnewski......Herman Eckel.
20...J. H. Rhodes..........James F. Fisher.

OFFICERS OF THE BOARD.

President, S. S. Fisher.
Vice-President, Francis Ferry.
Corresponding Secretary, James F. Irwin.
Clerk, W. F. Hurlbut.

OFFICERS OF THE SCHOOLS

Superintendent of Schools, John Hancock.
Superintendent of Buildings, John McCammon.

POST-OFFICE.

C. W. Thomas, Esq., the late efficient and popular Postmaster of Cincinnati, has kindly furnished some interesting items in regard to the business of his department:

As nearly every interest of a civilized people pulsates through the post-office, it undoubtedly furnishes the most reliable indication of numerical, commercial, and social progress. From a statement in the "Commercial Daily Advertiser," of November 19, 1829, we learn "there was received for postage the last year $12,150, having increased in three years upward of fifty per cent." This was when Cincinnati had a population of twenty-five thousand. She had outstripped all other Western cities, and was indisputably the "Queen." These figures afford an interesting comparison with the business done at the office during 1867–8.

The cash receipts of the Cincinnati Post-office, on postage account, were, for the past year, $264,587.47, and the expenses for salaries and miscellaneous, exclusive of those incident to the free-delivery system, were $62,306.06; net earnings paid over to the Government, $202,281.41.

The receipts and disbursements in the Money-Order Department of the office were each over half a million dollars. At the present rate of business, over

$750,000 will be paid on money orders during the present year.

The number of letters received for delivery during the past year was nine million three hundred and eight thousand, and the number received for distribution was twenty-eight million.

The amount of mail matter daily handled is about twenty-five thousand pounds. There are one hundred employés, including letter carriers, and the machinery of the office is incessant day and night.

It should be remembered, that in 1829, domestic postage on letters was 12½, 18¾, and 25 cents, according to the distance conveyed. That year's receipts, $12,150, would be equivalent to the transmission of sixty-four thousand eight hundred letters at the average of 18¾ cents each. The same sum will now convey four hundred and five thousand half-ounce letters to any distance within the United States; so the whole sum of $264,587.47, the postage receipts for the past year, fairly represents about nine millions of letters received by the people of this city.

THE ANNUAL MESSAGE

of Mayor Charles F. Wilstach, dated April 9, 1869, congratulates the city upon the enterprise and prosperity which has hitherto marked its career, and takes the most enlarged and comprehensive views of its future. It states the bonded debt of the city to be now $4,507,000, and the value of property belonging to the city at $11,350,000, showing nearly $7,000,000 on the right side of the ledger.

The following items in regard to some of the departments of the municipal government are taken from the message:

THE BOARD OF HEALTH.

The Board of Health has, during the past year, accomplished much that has been valuable to the health and comfort of the citizens. Through its officers, it has succeeded in ridding the markets of unwholesome meats and vegetables. It has prevented the sale of diseased cattle, and has required of the venders of milk the most rigid conformance to its rules against adulteration.

It also prevented the spread of that terrible scourge called the Texas cattle fever. The Health Officer, Dr. William Clendenin, was especially energetic in his endeavors to prevent its spread among the cattle of this vicinity. That these efforts were effectual, the results have abundantly proven.

The mortality in Cincinnati for the year ending February 28, 1869, was 4,684. The population of the city, being estimated at 260,000, would make the death rate 18.05 in 1,000 inhabitants. This is a remarkably low mortality, and clearly demonstrates the great salubrity of Cincinnati. In New York City, in 1868, the death rate was 32.27 in 1,000 inhabitants; in Brooklyn, the same year, it was 27.81; in Providence, in 1864, it was 23.50 in 1,000. In St. Louis, according to the last annual report of the Board of Health, for the year 1868, the mortality was 5,193; in Chicago, during the same period, the mortality was 4,604.

The mortality from particular diseases exhibits equally satisfactory results. For example, the mortality from consumption in Cincinnati during the year ending with February last, was 444, or 9.48 per cent. of the whole number of deaths in that time. The mortality from consumption in New York last year was 3,286, or 14.02 per centage on the total number of deaths. In Philadelphia, during the same period, the mortality from consumption was 1,947, or 15.38 per consumption during the year 1868, in St. Louis, were 503.

THE POLICE DEPARTMENT.

The Chief of Police, Captain James L. Ruffin, reports that the total number of arrests during the year, for all degrees of crimes, was 8,291, of which 6,734 were males and 1,557 females. In the lodging apartments of the different station-houses, there have been accommodated 25,000 persons, of whom 20,209 were males and 3,424 females; for safe keeping, 1,152; lost children returned to parents, 255; deserters arrested, 11; number of per-

LATTA'S STEAM FIRE ENGINE.

sons committed to the Work-house during the year, 1,176, of whom 1,037 were males and 139 females.

The Police Telegraph has sent, during the year, 4,092 messages, as follows: Lost children returned, 755; estrays returned, 290; wagons, buggies, etc., returned, 200; prisoners discharged from Work-house, 169; officers to suppress riots, 7; orders issued, 20; prisoners for court, 150; miscellaneous 2,555.

THE FIRE DEPARTMENT

still maintains its supremacy over any like department in existence, and is famed throughout the country for its efficiency and promptness in subduing the ravages of one of the fiercest elements of destruction known to the human race. Our city has enjoyed, during the past year, a marked immunity from large fires. New and powerful machines are being added to the present effective force, and nothing is left undone to render the department equal to the growth of the city and the demands of the citizens for the fullest protection.

Enoch G. Megrue, the veteran Chief of the Department, has continued to devote his entire energies to the discipline and management of the force.

The cost of the department for the past year has been $240,584.13. There have been 183 alarms and 90 actual fires during the year. Value of property destroyed,

$447,382.00, the insurance on which was $271,016.00—making the actual loss to property-owners $176,366.00.

ADMINISTRATION OF JUSTICE.

1. JUSTICES OF THE PEACE are elected by the voters of each township, for terms of three years. They have jurisdiction in all civil suits, with a few exceptions, when the debt or damages do not exceed three hundred dollars. In criminal cases they have jurisdiction throughout the county, of minor offenses, and to hold persons accused of crime to answer the charge in the Court of Common Pleas.

2. THE DISTRICT COURT is composed of the three judges of the Court of Common Pleas of Hamilton County, and one of the judges of the Supreme Court of Ohio, any three of whom constitute a quorum for the transaction of business. Two terms are held each year, commencing on the first Monday of April, and first Monday of October respectively. It has but little original jurisdiction, its business being chiefly the determination of appeals, and cases in error from the Court of Common Pleas.

3. THE COURT OF COMMON PLEAS is composed of three judges, elected by the people of Hamilton County, for a term of five years. The regular terms of the Court commence on the first Monday of January, the second

Monday of May, and the first Monday of November in
each year. The judges sit separately and alternately,
in each of the three rooms of the court. They have
authority, by statute, to classify and distribute among
themselves for trial the business pending in the court.
Civil cases are tried by the court in room No. 1, and
before a jury in room No. 2, and criminal cases are tried
in room No. 3. This court has original jurisdiction in
all civil cases where the sum or matter in dispute exceeds one hundred dollars, and has appellate jurisdiction from the judgment of justices of the peace, and
also in certain cases from the decisions of the county
commissioners. It has jurisdiction of all crimes and
offenses in which persons are indicted by the grand
jury; of all writs of certiorari to the Police Court and
justices of the peace in criminal cases; of petitions in
error from judgments rendered by the Probate Court or
justices of the peace; in cases of contested election of
county officers; and of petitions by administrators and
executors for the sale of lands of deceased persons, and
in habeas corpus. It also has powers and duties prescribed by statute, with reference to savings societies,
petitions filed by railroads for change of grade or route,
sales of property of religious societies; sales of cemeteries in cities and towns; changes of names of persons,
towns, and villages; vacation of town plats; appointment
of auctioneers, inspectors, etc.; sales of entailed estates;

barring dower of insane wives; appointment of various trustees; approval of appointment of deputies of the clerk, sheriff, and recorder, etc. The judges, whose terms will expire in 1872, are Hons. Charles C. Murdock, Joseph Cox, and Manning F. Force.

4. THE SUPERIOR COURT OF CINCINNATI consists of three judges, elected at city elections, by the voters of Cincinnati, for the term of five years. The terms of the court commence on the first Monday of each month, except July, August, and September. A special term of the court is held by each judge, and, as a general rule, the judges sit alternately in each of the three rooms of the court, submitted cases being heard in room No. 1, and jury cases in rooms No. 2 and 3. The general term is held at such time as the court may direct, by two or more judges, the concurrence of two being necessary to pronounce judgment at general term. Petitions in error lie from the special to the general terms, and from the general terms directly to the Supreme Court of the State. This court has no jurisdiction except that specially conferred upon it by statute. Generally it has, in civil actions, the same jurisdiction in the City of Cincinnati that the Court of Common Pleas has in the county of Hamilton. It has no jurisdiction of appeals or petitions in error from other tribunals, nor of criminal cases, nor of applications for divorce and alimony. At present, the judges are Hon. Bellamy Storer, whose term ex-

pires in 1872; Hon. M. B. Hagans, whose term expires in 1873; and Hon. Alphonso Taft, whose term expires in 1874.

5. THE PROBATE COURT, a court of record, open at all times, is holden by one judge, elected by the voters of the county for the term of three years. The Probate Judge is clerk of his own court, and his compensation is by fees fixed by law. He has jurisdiction in probate and testamentary matters; in the appointment of administrators and guardians; in the settlement of the accounts of executors, administrators, and guardians; in habeas corpus; in the issuing of marriage licenses; in sales of land, on petition of executors, administrators, and guardians; in the completion of contracts concerning real estate, on petition of executors and administrators; in holding inquests of lunacy; in ascertaining the amount of compensation to be made to owners of land appropriated to the use of corporations; to try contested elections of justices of the peace, and of proceedings in aid of execution. He also has authority to administer oaths, and to take depositions, and the acknowledgment of deeds, etc. The present incumbent is the Hon. Edw. F. Noyes.

6. THE POLICE COURT OF CINCINNATI is held by a police judge, elected by the voters of the city, for the term of two years. He has, in criminal cases, the same powers and jurisdiction as justices of the peace. He

has jurisdiction of all violations of the ordinances of the city, and of all cases of petit larceny and other inferior offenses committed within the limits of the city, or within one mile thereof, and which the constitution or laws of the State do not require to be prosecuted by indictment or presentment of a grand jury. In the absence, sickness, or other disability of the police judge, the mayor may select some reputable member of the bar, residing in the city, who may, after taking the necessary oath of office, preside in the police court as "acting police judge." Hon. Walter F. Straub is the present judge of this court.

7. The United States Courts held in the city of Cincinnati are the Circuit and District Courts for the Southern District of Ohio. The District Court is held by the District Judge, and has jurisdiction in cases in admiralty, in bankruptcy, of all seizures, of all suits for penalties and forfeitures, and of suits at common law by the United States, or any officer thereof. The Circuit Court consists of a judge of the Supreme Court assigned to the Circuit, and of the Judge of the District Court of the District. A recent statute provides for the appointment of an additional Circuit judge. The Circuit Court may be held by either of the judges. It has, in general, cognizance of crimes and offenses cognizable under the authority of the United States, and of suits of a civil nature, when the matter in dispute

exceeds five hundred dollars, exclusive of costs, and when the United States are plaintiffs, or an alien is a party, or the suit is between a citizen of the State and a citizen of another State. Justice N. H. Swayne, of the Supreme Court of the United States, and Hon. H. Leavitt, Judge of the District Court, are the present judges of the Circuit Court. Judges of the United States Courts hold their offices during good behavior.

CHAPTER VI.

THE nineteenth century can boast of no brighter glory than its Christian Charities. They distinguish it as the era of philanthropy, and, in their vast extent and ramifications, declare a nobler type of humanity and a higher civilization than any previous age has seen. The toilers of the Christian Commission were truer heroes than the exactors of Magna Charta; John Howard and Elizabeth Fry the apostles of a more glorious idea than that which made martyrs of Hampden and Sidney. Let history, then, set anew its stakes and cords, and mark well the track of the philanthropies which have made these later years an epoch in the progress of the race, and which make gloriously true the utterance, that "Peace hath her victories no less renowned than war."

The chronicles of the Charities of Cincinnati would, of themselves, require a volume. But a brief outline can here be given. There is exhibited a princely liberality in the support of these "inns upon the road of life, where **suffering humanity** finds alleviation and sympathy;" and all honor is due to those individuals who pass not **by unheeded** their pitiable fellow-mortals, **but are stretching forth** unceasingly the helping hand. These are **they who do not believe that misfortune is a** crime, but who, **recognizing the universal brotherhood of** humanity, **"walk the crowded streets with eyes keenly** alert to detect **the objects of suffering and sympathy** around them, and wait **not for the opportunity to be** pressed upon them, but *seek out* the opportunities which shall give **expression to the grand impulses of their** natures."

Let this be **counted a hopeful sign of the times, that** there is rapidly progressing **a skillful** adaptation of judicious charities **to the wants of** men, and that those heaven-born **words "Our Father,"** of which Madam De Staël said that if **Christ had simply** taught men to say them, he **would have been the greatest** benefactor of the race, **are gaining here, as elsewhere,** a new meaning in the minds of **earnest men.**

A reliable, **though necessarily brief, statement will** be given **in the following pages.** It is done in the hope that such **persons as are willing to bestow a portion of** their time and **wealth in a benevolent direction** may be able **to gain a knowledge of the special province** of each **institution.** It will be well if from many new sources **there come generous responses toward these in-**

stitutions of blessing, whose corps of workers is always open to recruits, and whose treasuries can never be too full. The greater prominence is given to what may be termed the voluntary Charities, unsectarian in their character, and maintained by voluntary contributions. The municipal institutions are mentioned subsequently. Laboring side by side with the common purpose of lightening the load of human misery, they are a shining sisterhood of mercy, a joy to the world.

CINCINNATI UNION BETHEL.

The Cincinnati Union Bethel was first established on the 27th of January, 1839. It owes its existence to the efforts of the Western Seamen's Friend Society, under whose control it was, with some intermission, from the above date until February, 1856, when it became an independent institution, incorporated under the general law of the State of Ohio.

The first record book states that, at its opening, on that date, there were present seven teachers and sixteen scholars; that the school was opened with prayer, led by Philip Hinkle; and that it commenced its missionary labors by inciting the zeal of the scholars in a promise to record, on the minutes, the name of the scholar who brought in the most children on the next Sunday. The week following, the minutes of the school showed that John Ryland and John M. Jones each brought two new scholars, and that William Harrison brought two as far as the door—"one came in, out the other ran off."

Since the period of this simple, life-like record, the Bethel has passed through many changes—at times being suspended, and at others abandoned. It was then a tenant at will in the location now occupied, was frequently driven from place to place in search of a home, until, in the year 1852, it entered upon a new and more permanent career. The citizens of Cincinnati placed at the disposal of the Western Seamen's Friend Society, means sufficient to build the well-known Floating Bethel, which was occupied until the year 1859. In that Chapel, in the year 1854, the Bethel School, which has continued without interruption since, was gathered by Rev. S. D. Clayton; was carried on under his direction until 1857; from 1857 to 1859, under the management of Rev. Wm. Andrews; and in the fall of 1859 was removed from the Floating Bethel to its present location on the wharf. Subsequently, the school has passed into the charge of Benjamin Frankland, and with the exception of the two years, from 1859 to 1861, when Mr. Clayton was again the efficient Chaplain, the entire Bethel work was under his general supervision.

Under Mr. Frankland's care, it accomplished wouderful results, and reached the height of a successful career. Thomas Lee is now Superintendent, and a new future of prosperity is opening.

The object and organization of the Bethel are presented in the following extracts from the Constitution:

This Association shall be known as the CINCINNATI UNION BETHEL.

The object shall be to provide for the spiritual and temporal welfare of river-men and their families, and all others who may be unreached by regular church organizations; to gather in and furnish religious instruction and material aid to the poor and neglected children of Cincinnati and vicinity, and to make such provisions as may be deemed best for their social elevation; *also*, to provide homes and employment for the destitute.

Any person paying into the treasury of the corporation the sum of ten dollars, shall be a member for one year, and of fifty dollars, a member for life.

There shall be a Board of Directors, to consist of twelve persons, four of whom shall retire each year, and their successors shall be elected at the annual meeting, to serve for the term of three years.

The Board shall appoint from their own number a committee of five, to be called the Property Committee, whose duty it shall be to supervise and manage all real estate, of which the corporation may at any time become the possessors, and all moneys or property which may be donated or bequeathed for the endowment of said corporation, under direction of the Board.

All operations of the Union shall be conducted upon the basis of a union of all Christian denominations.

No debt shall ever be contracted by the Board of Directors which will encumber the property of the corporation.

It shall not be in the power of the members of the Society at any meeting, or of the officers thereof, to divert the property of the institution, real or personal, from the distinct purposes provided for in these articles, but the same shall forever remain to fulfill the object of the Society, as herein defined, and for no other purpose whatever.

The Bethel work, at this time, embraces the following departments:

1. The River Mission, among boatmen, etc.
2. Systematic Visitation of Families.
3. The Bethel Church.
4. The Bethel School.
5. The Relief Department.
6. The Sewing School.
7. The Free Reading and Cheap Dining Hall.
8. The Newsboys' Home.

The details of the various branches of the work are placed, by the constitution, in the hands of an executive committee, composed of three members of the Board, and the Secretary of the Society.

The annual report of the Secretary, Dr. J. Taft, made in March, 1869, furnishes the following interesting facts in regard to these departments. They will make the best exhibit of the varied work of this noble institution.

THE BETHEL CHURCH.—Services have been held regularly each Sabbath, morning and evening, and each Wednesday evening a social prayer meeting has met. Extra meetings in January and February, under the ministrations of Rev. Thomas Lee, resulted in an accession to the church of twenty persons.

THE RIVER MISSION.—We have, as in the past, endeavored to carry on active work among the boatmen and laborers that throng our wharf, by missionary visitation to the boat, the distribution of tracts, and welcome to the services of the Bethel.

THE BETHEL SCHOOL has not only sustained its previous reputation for numbers and interest, but has considerably exceeded the last report. The averages of attendance of scholars for the several months have been as follows:

1868—March, 1,630; April, 1,350; May, 920; June, 920; July, 700; August, 750; September, 850; October, 1,250; November, 1,850; December, 1,970. 1869—January, 1,940; February, 2,000.

Since the 1st of November last the actual attendance

of scholars has exceeded 1,800 on sixteen Sabbaths; has exceeded 1,900 on eight Sabbaths; and has exceeded 2,000 on four Sabbaths. The highest attendance was on February 21, when the number of scholars present was 2,248.

The usual attendance in the boys' infant class is about 350; the girls, 300. We have fully 200 scholars over eighteen years of age.

The indications of the accomplishment of great good in this department are so manifest and abundant as to constitute a source of great gratification.

THE RELIEF DEPARTMENT is carried on under the special direction of the Ladies' Union Bethel Aid Society.

From the report of Mrs. J. W. Canfield, their Secretary, are compiled the following statistics:

The number of distributions of clothing held during the year was twenty-nine, at which 2,782 articles of made clothing were given away; also 1,388 yards of white muslin, 3,862 yards of calico, and 803 yards of cloth for boys' wear.

Embraced in the above are the following items of separate articles, and numbers given: Shoes, 750 pairs; hose, 140 pairs; hoods, 84; caps, 234; jackets, 61; shawls, 63; skirts, 10; comforts, 55; girls' hats, 100; aprons, 79; shirts, 159; pants, 90; dresses, 69; under-garments, 190.

In addition to these regular clothing distributions, almost hourly calls at the Bethel for assistance have been patiently inquired into, and, when deemed worthy, and the means at our disposal have justified it, relief has been given.

SEWING SCHOOL.—Intimately connected with the above department of the work, is the Mothers' Sewing School, which, during the most of the winter, has met, each Wednesday afternoon, at the Bethel building, under the direction of a committee of the Ladies' Bethel Aid Society. It numbers eighty-four members.

The following materials have been made into garments by the women attending; calico, 587½ yards; muslin, 222¾ yards; flannel, 126¾ yards.

This movement has been very successful, the time occupied by the women in sewing being improved by the reading of interesting and profitable selections from books and magazines, and in giving practical advice in matters of domestic economy.

NEWSBOYS' HOME.—Three thousand six hundred and fifty night lodgings have been furnished to boys—newsboys and boot-blacks—and about seven thousand five hundred meals, at a nominal price of ten cents each.

In September, Mr. and Mrs. Leonard Worcester, who, for more than a year, had charge of this department, left us to enter a missionary field in the Indian Territory. From that time, Mr. C. B. Taylor, of Lane Seminary, superintended the newsboys' department. He also, for some three months, successfully carried on a night school for boys, with an average attendance of twenty-two.

THE COFFEE AND READING ROOM.—This has been successfully continued, and is fulfilling the purpose of its establishment, not only by furnishing a cheap and substantial meal, without any of the objectionable associations too often found in boatmen's boarding houses, but as a direct means of promoting frugality, temperance, and practical religion. The number of persons daily availing themselves of its advantages is about three hundred.

While it is self-sustaining, it really proves, from the low rates charged, a great help to many whose means are limited, and it attracts to our institution a large number of just the class of people that we are desirous should become acquainted with the other features of our work. The following bill of fare, etc., will give an idea of the arrangements:

BILL OF FARE.

Coffee or Tea, with Crackers or Bread, . .	5 cts.
Milk, ...	5 cts.
Butter, ...	5 cts.
Doughnuts, ...	5 cts.
Pie, ...	5 cts.
Soup, with Crackers or Bread, ...	5 cts.

9

Cold Meat, ... 5 cts.

Roast Meat and Potatoes, ... 10 cts.

Pork and Beans, ... 10 cts.

Other articles in proportion.

Dinner Tickets, . . . 25 Cents,

For which will be furnished Roast Meat and Vegetables, Pie,

Coffee, Bread, and Butter.

Dinner from 12 to 2 o'clock.

The rooms are open from six A. M. to eight P. M. The free reading room is supplied with daily and weekly papers, and other reading matter.

The importance of a suitable building had long been felt, and, in 1868, the foundation of a noble edifice was laid. Its estimated cost is sixty thousand dollars, and the plan provides for the following departments:

1. A grand hall, with class and anterooms, capable of holding two thousand five hundred people, or three thousand children, to be used for the sessions of the Bethel School, meetings and lectures, religious and otherwise, and for night schools for the working classes.

2. A temperance eating establishment, where, with cheerful and pleasant surroundings, the boatman and laboring man can obtain a cheap meal, without resorting to drinking saloons.

3. A free reading room, accessible at all times, and supplied with choice and entertaining reading matter.

4. Dormitories, airy and clean, for boatmen, poor strangers, and children who may need temporary shelter.

5. A people's bath and wash-house, conducted upon such plan as will reach the wants of all.

6. A workingmen's gymnasium.

7. Rooms for relief department and uses of Ladies' Bethel Aid Society.

8. A newsboys' home.

There will be a hall seventy-five by eighty-six feet, the height of the ceiling being forty feet.

The plan proposes a wide entrance-way from Front Street, and two entrances from Yeatman Street. Spacious galleries are to occupy three sides of the audience room, the space underneath being divided into Bible and infant class rooms, separated by sliding glass doors. It will probably be the most complete hall of the kind in the country, and, for school purposes, will accommodate four thousand children.

Thus is the Cincinnati Bethel faithfully fulfilling its noble trust. A pure and lofty purpose, a catholic spirit, and far-reaching charity make it a mighty agency for good. The entire community owe to it a debt of gratitude that should find its expression in substantial tokens.

Officers.

BOARD OF DIRECTORS.

John Gates, *President.*	Philip Hinkle, *Vice-Pres.*
C. R. Lewis, *Treasurer.*	J. Taft, *Secretary.*
L. E. Stevens,	A. Judson Davis,

M. M. White,   A. Erkenbrecher,
C. H. Gould,   Abner L. Frazer.
        W. B. Moores.

EXECUTIVE COMMITTEE.

C. H. Gould,   M. M. White,
Chas. R. Lewis,   J. Taft, *Ex-officio*.

PROPERTY COMMITTEE.

Philip Hinkle,   L. E. Stevens,
C. H. Gould,   Andrew Erkenbrecher,
        W. B. Moores.

AUDITING COMMITTEE.

C. H. Gould,   Abner L. Frazer.

GENERAL SUPERINTENDENT.

Rev. Thomas Lee.

BETHEL CHURCH (*Undenominational*).

Rev. Thomas Lee, *Pastor*.

BETHEL SCHOOL.

Rev. Thomas Lee, *Superintendent*.
Philip Hinkle, *Assistant Superintendent*.
J. Taft,   "   "
John Gates,   "   "
C. R. Lewis, *Secretary*.

Cincinnati Union Bethel, Nos. 30 and 31, Public
Landing.

FORM OF BEQUEST.

I give and bequeath to "The Cincinnati Union Bethel," a Corporation created in the year eighteen hundred and sixty-five, under the laws of the State of Ohio, or to the Treasurer thereof, for the time being, for its corporate purposes, the sum of ——— dollars.

FORM OF DEVISE OF REAL ESTATE.

I give and devise to "The Cincinnati Union Bethel," a Corporation created in the year eighteen hundred and sixty-five, under the laws of the State of Ohio, or to the Treasurer thereof, for the time being, for its corporate purposes, all that, etc. (Here describe the property.)

CINCINNATI ORPHAN ASYLUM.

No class of suffering humanity more tenderly appeals to the heart of benevolence, or more readily enlists the sympathy and kindness of men, than orphans. Not only does their destitute and helpless condition awaken pity, but their forming minds and impressible natures seem to invite the power of good influences to shape and mold them into beings who shall ornament society and bless the world. It was thus that they early became the objects of philanthropical effort. Early in the history of Cincinnati this method of charity began to enlist attention, and the result was the pioneer charity of the Queen City, the Cincinnati Orphan Asylum.

This beneficent institution is now in the thirty-sixth

year of its corporate existence. One of the earliest
organized Charities in the State of Ohio, it has steadily
pursued its object of caring for that class of children
whose misfortunes appeal so strongly to their fellow-
mortals. For many years it was the only Protestant
institution in the city which offered relief and shelter to
those of tender years. It had its origin in a previously
existing society of ladies who had in view the circulation of Bibles and the general relief of the poor. In
1833, a charter was obtained, and in 1836, a commodious
building was erected upon Elm Street, north of Twelfth,
sufficient to meet the growing demands of the Society.
Prominently identified with its early history are the
names of Mrs. Judge Burnet, Mrs. Samuel Cloon, Mrs.
Catherine Bates, Mrs. Samuel W. Davies, Mrs. Stille,
and others. The arms of its generous ministrations were
stretched widely to embrace every class of suffering
and neglected children. The establishment, in later
years, of kindred institutions in a different field, left
the Orphan Asylum to carry out its primary intention
and to devote all its means and energies to orphans
alone.

In 1861, the Elm Street property having been sold,
the structure now occupied on Mt. Auburn was erected.
The location is a delightful one, comprising ample
grounds and commanding an extensive view of the city,
Ohio River, and the distant hills. The building is a

spacious brick edifice, three stories, with basement and tower. Suitable apartments are provided, the best ventilation secured, and every provision made for the comfort and health of the inmates. The regulations provide for a Board of Managers, consisting of twelve ladies. They are elected agreeably to the charter every three years. A duly appointed committee exercise discretion in regard to the admission of children. All applicants are examined by the attending physician. A binding committee superintend the placing of children in homes. No child is to be placed with any one who keeps a hotel, tavern, or coffee house, nor with any one who does not regularly attend religious worship. The relatives and friends of the children are allowed to visit them on the first Wednesday in every two months, and at other times only by special permission of the managers.

The laws of the institution are formed with a careful regard to the present and future well-being of the orphans. No child can be taken out of the asylum until it has remained there at least one year, so that vicious habits may be corrected before they mingle with society. The strictest scrutiny is made into the character of individuals who apply for children. Stipulations are made as to the amount of education they shall receive. When a child leaves the institution, a manager is appointed as its guardian, to whom, in case of grievance, it may apply for redress, and look for protection.

Every attention is given to the moral and mental training of the children. Regular religious services and Sabbath school instruction are provided, while, during the week, those of sufficient age attend the city Public Schools. The present Matron is Miss Jennie Watson, assisted by her sister, Miss Belle Watson. Dr. C. D. Palmer is physician in charge. The cost of conducting the institution is about $15,000 per annum. Of this, the endowment fund yields an annual revenue of about eight thousand dollars. This leaves about the same amount to be contributed by the benevolent people of Cincinnati and its vicinity.

The Thirty-fifth Annual Report, made in 1868, states the whole number of children admitted, since the founding of the institution, to be 16,053. There are about 100 inmates at present.

What a history of benefaction do the annals of this institution present! Who shall define the ever-widening circles of its precious influence? As long as useful men and women have a work to do; as long as a happy home gathers about its name the dearest associations of human existence, so long shall this shelter and comfort of the orphan continue to receive the countenance and support of the dispensers of charity. The fifth decade of its history should be one of signal prosperity.

Officers.

Mrs. Catherine Bates, *President.*
Mrs. Eliza J. Funk, *Vice-President.*
Miss Janet C. Brown, *Recording Secretary.*
Mrs. John Davis, *Corresponding Secretary.*
Mrs. John Shillito, *Treasurer.*

Managers.

Mrs. J. P. Harrison,	Mrs. Henry Probasco,
" J. D. Jones,	" S. J. Broadwell,
" A. D. Bullock,	" A. S. Winslow,
" M. F. Thompson,	" G. H. Barbour,
" J. H. Cheever,	" G. T. Stedman,
" A. F. Perry,	" William Hooper,

Mrs. C. T. H. Stille.

CINCINNATI RELIEF UNION.

This noble organization was established in 1848.
Prominent among its originators was Rev. James H.
Perkins, whose benevolent efforts in Cincinnati are
matters of history. It is regularly incorporated, and
has for its sole mission the temporary relief of the
worthy and destitute poor of the city without distinction of religion, nationality, or color. It is altogether
dependent on voluntary contributions. As often as

appealed to, a generous community has responded with funds. A Board of Managers, composed of members from each ward, gratuitously devote much time and care, and have given it years of experience. The design of the institution is:

The prevention of vagrancy and street-begging;

The diminution of imposition upon the benevolent;

Advice and instruction to all as to some honest means of procuring a livelihood;

The placing of the young in secular and Sabbath schools;

The relief of those who are known to need it, by gifts of food, fuel, clothing, and other actual necessaries.

The expenditures of the institution for a period of twelve months, from November 8, 1866, to November 9, 1867, show an aggregate of relief dispensed of $34,000, prudently distributed in provisions, shoes, clothing, fuel, and other necessaries, to the needy and worthy poor of Cincinnati.

To properly carry out the above objects, the institution is organized as follows:

There are several managers or directors for every ward in the city, whose duty it is to become acquainted with the condition of those families in the ward tha require assistance; and, to more effectually carry out this provision, it is considered the duty of the managers to visit the families at their residences.

A Board of Control meets weekly during the winter season, and once a month the balance of the year.

There is a Central Office, where the goods purchased for distribution are stored, and where the orders of the Ward Directors are filled. The office is open every afternoon, except Sundays, during the winter season, from 2 to 4 o'clock, for the transaction of business.

The Relief Union has the highest claims, and should be cordially sustained by the citizens.

Its method of distributing relief is admitted to be the best of any system of charity now in vogue, combining simplicity with great economy. It is managed by gentlemen who serve gratuitously, and whose only motive is to do good. The whole expenses of the institution, for several years, have averaged less than $300 per year.

No money is distributed except in extreme cases, the means of the institution being invested in goods, purchased at the lowest rates.

By the thorough system of visitation and inquiry adopted by the managers, the relief goes where it is most needed. The directors are familiar with the wants of the poor of our city, and are also familiar with the means generally adopted by impostors and the unworthy to impose on the benevolent.

Indiscriminate giving of charity is injurious, and encourages vagrancy and street-begging. Many of the persons who solicit charity in the streets are unworthy of assistance. By supplying the Relief Union with abundant means each year, the subscribers to this great charity fund can be assured, with all confidence, that the really needy and worthy will be properly assisted when in distress.

The name of C. W. Starbuck will stand upon the records of this munificent charity as that of "one who loved his fellow-men." Its success in late years has been largely due to his efforts.

The office of the Relief Union is in the City Buildings.

Officers.

Rev. J. Chester, *President.*   S. S. Davis, *Treasurer.*
J. C. Morrison, *Vice-Pres.*   Alex. Aupperle, *Secretary.*

Managers.

WARD.

1...E. Evans.................Wm. Haller.
2...George C. Miller......R. Allison.
3...H. Kiersted............Wm. Clark, J. C. Morrison.
4...J. E. Vansant.
5...G. H. Dean ....John H. Balance.
6...Ira Wood...............Henry Stauffer, Sam. Stokes.
7...Samuel Blair ....J. F. Leuchtenburg.
8...R. B. Moore............Hugh Pugh, A. Carnes.
9...F. Beresford............J. Feldwisch.
10...Jos. Siefert.............Isaac Wieser.

11...R. Bieman................M. B. Masson.
12...John F. Forbus.......C. V. Bechman, Geo. Scheu.
13...Dr. M. Lilienthal.....John T. Jones.
14...John Webb, Jr ....Benjamin Groff.
15...C. W. Starbuck ....Carter Cook.
16...Wm. H. King.........Hiram Pugh.
17...Milton Glenn..........H. Janes.
18...Rev. J. Chester........H. W. Taylor.
19...Alex. Aupperle ....John Whetstone.
20...Thos. Asbury..........Samuel Beresford.

CHILDREN'S HOME.

The idea of the reformation and training of neglected children is of comparatively recent development. Christian philanthropy had long been accomplishing a noble work in other directions before Raikes, wiser than he knew, initiated the movement which has grown into the vast system of juvenile reformation now existing. The philosophy is correct—the twig may be bent where all effort will fail to change the tree. Murray Shipley had long been actively engaged in this department of labor in Cincinnati, when, in 1860, the initiatory steps were taken by him in a new and noble enterprise.

It was found that a portion of the city, south of Fourth and west of Plum, was almost destitute of religious instruction. It embraced over thirty squares, closely populated, in which were many tenement houses, rookeries, and shanties, and included one ward of the city noted as a resort for large numbers of regular thieves and abandoned characters.

The need being felt of some evangelizing influence, a cellar-room on Mill Street, below Third, was rented, and there was commenced the Penn Mission Sabbath School. The children were of the rudest and roughest character. The numbers were limited to the capacity of the room, about seventy; but in November, 1863, a three-story brick building having been erected on Park Street, with a large hall in the third story, fitted up for meetings and Sabbath Schools, a removal was made, and the school at once increased to an attendance of three hundred.

The Children's Home of Cincinnati was incorporated December 12, 1864. The work had been previously carried on by the President, Murray Shipley, and the majority of the present lady managers. There were then a superintendent and matron employed, and thirteen children in the Home.

Experience having shown that the boys received who were over twelve years of age needed to be *trained* into habits of industry, an appeal to our citizens met with a ready response, and $20,000 was subscribed. As a result, in the spring of 1867, a farm of seventy-five acres, on College Hill, about eight miles from the city, was purchased, and is now in successful operation. This is the Children's Home School Farm.

A Branch Home, on East Sixth Street, with a day school, was established in January, 1868. There are then, *three departments:*

1st. The Home, 19 and 21 Park Street, where the children live, and its day school.

2d. The School Farm, for older boys. A similar provision for girls is in contemplation.

3d. Branch No. 1, East Sixth Street, and its day school.

Religious services of various kinds are held on Sunday and during the week. The Penn Mission Sabbath School, on Park Street, and the Grellet Mission School, on Sixth Street, have each an enrollment of about five hundred.

The institution aims to ameliorate and elevate the condition of the children of poor and unfortunate parents:

1st. By procuring for the homeless and destitute who may be committed to it, in accordance with its charter, permanent country homes in Christian families, where they shall be trained in habits of industry, and receive a suitable English education. They are clothed, fed, and instructed gratuitously as long as they remain in the institution.

2d. By affording a temporary home to poor children, whose parents, thus aided, may be enabled to support them in a short time in homes of their own.

3d. By rescuing from the education of the streets, so ruinous in its effects, many who, for the want of clothing, books, etc., do not attend the Public Schools.

The following are some of the conditions in regard to applicants for children to be placed in homes.

The applicant must live in the country, and is required to be a member of some Evangelical Christian Church.

He is to agree to take the child into his family, clothe and feed it comfortably, give it good common school education, so as to enable it to enter creditably on the ordinary duties of life.

4th. He is to agree to train it up, so far as he is able, in the precepts of virtue and the Christian religion.

Parties having children will be expected to report to the Superintendent every three months.

A cordial invitation is extended to all to visit "The Home," at 19 and 21 Park Street.

In 1868, one hundred and fifty-nine children were received into the Home, and one hundred and fourteen were provided with homes in the country. Thus the grand work is going on, and hundreds of useful men and women will hereafter rise up and pronounce blessed this noble charity.

The Trustees of the Institution for 1869 are—

    Murray Shipley, *President.*

    O. N. Bush, *Treasurer.*

    B. Homans, Jr., *Secretary.*

S. S. Fisher,	W. H. Doane,
Wm. Woods,	Larz Anderson,
John Shillito,	G. H. Lounsbery,

H. Thane Miller.

Lady Managers.

Mary J. Taylor,	Mary S. Johnson,
Hannah D. Shipley,	Harriet D. Bush,
Hannah P. Smith,	Aurelia S. Fisher,
Lydia S. Bateman,	Cornelia B. Marsh,
Elizabeth L. Taylor,	Caroline Bruce,

Priscilla Jones.

FORM OF BEQUEST.

I give and bequeath to the Children's Home of Cincinnati, Ohio, the sum of ———— Dollars, to be paid to the Treasurer, for the time being, for the use of said Association.

THE GERMAN PROTESTANT ORPHAN ASYLUM

was chartered in 1849. A structure of ample dimensions was erected upon Highland Avenue, Mt. Auburn, to which extensive additions have recently been made. The aims and modes of operation of this institution are similar to those of the Cincinnati Asylum.

The institution is under the superintendence of Rev. G. F. Pfafflin and Mrs. Mary Pfafflin. Under their able and careful management, the Asylum has enjoyed most encouraging prosperity.

10

Children of members of the Association are admitted though they may have lost but one parent; in other cases, only those who are bereaved of both parents.

At such times as are deemed proper, the children are placed in families, who obligate themselves to retain them until they arrive at their majority, at which time the boys are to receive two hundred dollars and the girls one hundred dollars in cash.

Coöperating with the institution, is the Ladies' Protestant Orphan Association, that furnishes all the clothing for the children.

The present improvements will cost thirty thousand dollars, and will accommodate one hundred additional children.

HOME FOR THE FRIENDLESS.

This praiseworthy charity, the object of which is the reclamation of abandoned females, is under the direction and management of ladies connected with the different Protestant Churches of the city. The Board of Managers includes benevolent women who move in the highest circles of the city, and who deserve honor for their persevering efforts in behalf of an unfortunate class that are regarded by many, though unjustly, as beyond the hope of redemption. An act of incorporation was obtained in 1860.

The constitution provides as follows:

This Society shall be called "The Protestant Home for the Friendless and Female Guardian Society."

The object of this Society shall be to seek out and provide a home for destitute females who, having forsaken the path of virtue, or having fallen into the hands of the betrayer, desire to return from their evil way, and again become respectable members of society. And it shall be the duty of the Society to guard virtuous females (who may seek temporary protection in the Home) from the snares of vice, by aiding them in every laudable way to obtain an honest livelihood and avoid temptation. It shall be its duty also to provide temporarily for destitute children, and, whenever practicable, to secure for them permanent homes in respectable families.

The affairs of the Society shall be controlled by fifteen managers, to be elected, as far as practicable, to represent the various Protestant denominations.

Any person paying the sum of from three dollars to five dollars yearly subscription shall be entitled to a membership in this institution, and each donor of twenty dollars, at any one time, shall be a member for life.

The work of these noble women who are thus, through this institution, bringing so many each year from loathsome to virtuous lives, is a glorious one. Many who enter the walls of the Home to attempt reformation become good women, and finally become useful members of society.

The following are statistical items from the last report:

Number admitted during the year, 163; of these returned to parents or friends, 23; provided with situations, 52; sent to hospital, 29; dismissed at their own request, 3; dismissed for bad behavior, 2; died, 3; admitted for transient rest, 44.

For several years the want of accommodations was strongly felt. Funds were raised, and in September, 1868, the corner-stone of a new building was laid. This edifice was formally opened in April, 1869. It is located on Court Street, between Central Avenue and John. The Home is a handsome structure of brick, with stone trimmings, fifty-four feet front, and four stories high. The internal arrangements are admirable. There is a roomy chapel, dormitories, and all needful accommodations for one hundred and fifty inmates.

Officers.

Mrs. Bellamy Storer, *President.*
   " R. M. Bishop,   } *Vice-Presidents.*
   " W. B. Chapman, }
   " Sarah Frankland, *Corresponding Secretary.*
   " M. M. White, *Recording Secretary.*
   " C. F. Bradley, *Treasurer.*

Managers.

Mrs. R. M. Bishop,	Mrs. Cyrus Mendenhall,
" C. F. Bradley,	" Wm. H. Malone,
" W. B. Chapman,	" B. F. Richardson,
" Sarah Frankland,	" Bellamy Storer,
" Richard Gray,	" Mary J. Taylor,
" G. Mendenhall,	" M. M. White,

Mrs. J. F. White.

Trustees.

R. M. Bishop, *President.*   Joseph Kinsey, *Vice-Prest.*
S. S. Davis, *Treasurer.*   B. F. Brannan, *Secretary.*

Robert Moore.

Mrs. Geo. H. Smith, *Matron.*

Miss M. A. Cunningham, *Asst. Matron.*

FORM OF BEQUEST.

I give and bequeath unto the PROTESTANT HOME FOR THE FRIENDLESS AND FEMALE GUARDIAN SOCIETY OF CINCINNATI, OHIO, the sum of ——, to be paid to the Treasurer, for the time being, for the use of said association.

LADIES UNION AID SOCIETY.

The object of this Society is to relieve the destitute sick and the deserving poor, without regard to color, and render aid to suffering humanity in general. It has been in operation but a few years, but has already done a noble work.

The number of persons who received assistance in 1867, nearly all of whom had aid each week during the winter, were six hundred and fifty-six.

Clothing and provisions distributed, were as follows:

Calico, 1,006 yards; flannel, 1,186 yards; muslin, 1,096 yards; jeans, 246 yards; burlaps, 368 yards; blankets, 72; comforts, 23; drawers, 109 pairs; stockings, 310 pairs; underclothing, 111; shirts, 45; shoes, 65; dresses, 61; skirts, 44; sacks, 6; hoods, etc., 10; hats and caps, 9; boots, 3 pairs; vests, 19; thread, 404 spools; bread tickets, 294; corn-meal, 1,276 quarts; hominy, 475 quarts; beans, 519 quarts; potatoes, 4 bushels; bacon, etc., 12.

The officers are:

Mrs. H. C. Whitman, *President.*
Mrs. Nathan Guilford, Sen., *Vice-President.*
Miss L. Vallette, *Treasurer.*
Mrs. A. L. Ryder, *Secretary.*

Managers.

Miss M. L. Harrison,	Mrs. Henchman.
Mrs. Charles Graham,	Miss L. Vallette,
" R. B. Field,	Mrs. William Woods,
" J. P. Whiteman,	" Bellows,
" W. J. Sampson,	" J. E. Stevenson,
" E. D. Wilder,	" J. Paul,
" Wesley Taylor,	" E. W. Guilford,

Mrs. H. S. Applegate,	Mrs. H. C. Whitman,
" William Coolidge,	" A. L. Ryder,
" Pitts Harrison,	" N. Guild,
" William Sumner,	" S. B. Brown,
" Dr. Richardson,	" J. B. Bruce.

FOWELL BUXTON MISSION SABBATH SCHOOL.

Officers.

H. B. Baily, *Supt.*	Levi C. Goodale, *Assistant.*
Wm. Browne, *Treas.*	Wm. I. Gray, "

Geo. B. Frost, *Secretary.*

John T. Bateman, Cyrus Mendenhall, Dr. Wm. Storer
How, *Executive Committee.*

This mission originated in January, 1865, beginning
with twenty-eight scholars and three teachers.

Its name was taken from that of Sir Thomas Fowell
Buxton, a prominent leader of Emancipation, in England.

The objects are:

To gather in the neglected and destitute colored
children of our city; to teach them the truths of the
Christian religion, to the saving of their souls, and to
relieve the physical suffering of those requiring aid.

To accomplish this, they are furnished with Bibles,
New Testaments, Sabbath School books and papers,

for their attendance, and the *very* needy are supplied with clothing, *after personal visitation.*

To help to raise the down-trodden, to impart a love of truth and virtue, to aid to self-respect, to help to educate into law-abiding citizens, must be to secure the sympathy of the Christian public every-where. To perform it efficiently, they are dependent, to a great extent, on the coöperation and sympathies, not only of Christian philanthropists, but of a generous community.

The average attendance during the year has been three hundred and forty-three scholars, the highest being six hundred and twelve. There are on active duty forty-four teachers and assistants.

These represent different denominations.

ST. LUKE'S HOSPITAL.

The object of this institution is to afford medical and surgical aid and nursing to sick and disabled persons, by a hospital and other appropriate means, and also to provide such persons with the ministrations of the Gospel.

The Hospital is located on the south-west corner of Franklin Street and Broadway. The Association was incorporated in January, 1866, with Henry Probasco, William Proctor, and Thomas G. Odiorne as Trustees.

The constitution provides that this Association shall

be called "St. Luke's Hospital Association of the Protestant Episcopal Church in the City of Cincinnati, Ohio," and has the following provisions:

The Bishop of the Protestant Episcopal Church of the Diocese of Ohio shall be the President of this Association, and the Assistant Bishop First Vice-President. The other officers shall be three Vice-Presidents, a Treasurer, and a Secretary, to be elected from and by a Board of thirty-three Managers, who, together with the said President and the members of the Board of Council and Advice, shall be denominated "The Board of Managers," any seven of whom shall be a quorum for the transaction of business.

The rectors and city missionaries of the Protestant Episcopal Church in Cincinnati and its vicinity shall, together with the President of the Association and the First Vice-President, constitute a Board, to be denominated the "Board of Council and Advice," to whom shall be committed all matters touching the religious ministrations of this Association, and of all institutions connected therewith.

Every person who shall contribute the sum of $5, annually, to this Association, shall be a member thereof, and every person contributing a sum not less than $500 shall be a life member thereof.

The following extracts are made from the reports of the Board of Managers:

In 1865, it was determined that we should no longer neglect to provide a hospital for the sick poor of all classes, with the best medical treatment, and to afford a suitable refuge and consolation, in sickness, for Protestant Christians and all others who would choose the benefits of such an institution. The intention was to begin with a few beds, and to carefully increase them as the means offered, until thirty beds should be supported. The building on the corner of Broadway and Franklin Streets, with twenty-eight rooms, the lot one hundred feet front on Broadway by ninety feet on Franklin Street, was leased, with the privilege of purchase at $15,000. Very soon the applicants for admission became so numerous that an immediate increase of beds was called for, and was promptly met by the benevolent societies of our churches, and thirty-six beds were occupied. It was also intended to provide *a free dispensary* for the poor outside of the house.

The managers have kept in mind that this hospital must minister moral and religious support to the minds of the suffering, as well as bodily cure; and it is intended to use every effort to make this most important part of the work more efficient. Devoted Christian women will be accepted, and encouraged to engage as voluntary laborers for Christ's sake, in this most noble work, systematically and with constancy of purpose.

In admission, there has been no respect to persons on

account of creed. Of two hundred and thirty patients admitted in 1866, the first year of the existence of the Hospital, only *thirty* were Protestant Episcopalians. All the patients have had the privilege of calling in their own religious teachers at any time they desired.

The sacred character of the ministrations, of the gentle influences enjoyed by those who are nursed in an institution like this, of the awakening of their moral sensibilities, and of the evidences of their physical and spiritual improvement, renders it impossible to exhibit completely its results and benefits in a brief sketch; and so the most interesting facts can only be made public by those who, with gladdened hearts, restored in mind and body, are continually passing out from its quiet wards.

Thousands of people in Cincinnati have already seen, and know of, the substantial benefits which have been dispensed in the last three years. Its growth has been quiet, but not secret; and it promises well to shine as a bright object among the many dark things in our large city. Hundreds have gone out testifying, with tears of thankfulness, to the Christian charity that raised them up to life and happiness.

Accomplished Christian ladies, who have means of support independently of the Hospital Association, and who have been thoroughly trained in the art of nursing and conducting a hospital properly, reside in the institution, and work gratuitously, superintending it, and receiving no remuneration. These are independent Protestant Sisters, devoting their whole time in Christian charity to beneficent work. Benevolent ladies ot distinction, and of high social and intellectual culture, are now in many places bending their energies to this noble and elevated sacrifice—devoting their superior qualities of mind and heart to the best interests of mankind and of Christianity.

No one connected with the hospital receives any payment for what they do for it, excepting the physician who resides in the hospital, under the direction of the medical and surgical staff, and some subordinate employés.

Persons who are sick and are able to pay for nursing, may have suitable accommodation in the rooms of the hospital, and be treated by their own physician, under the rules; and those who may be strangers here, and unexpectedly fall sick, or those who might be otherwise inconveniently situated in a hotel or boarding house, and require the best care, can find it here.

By paying $300 for a year, or by endowment in trust of $3,000, benevolent societies or persons may support or endow a single bed, and have the privilege of sending a patient to occupy it for a year, or permanently.

The extent of operations of this institution is continually widening, and it is hoped that, at no distant day, the funds will be raised to erect a commodious edifice for its use.

The following items are from the regulations:

Application for admission of patients may be made at the hospital, or to any member of the Executive Committee. Patients will be admitted without reference to their religion, and may be visited by clergymen of their own selection.

No cases of contagious diseases are admitted. Chronic or incurable cases will be retained no longer than medical treatment and nursing are essential to the relief or amelioration of suffering.

The friends of patients are admitted from $10\frac{1}{2}$ to 12 A. M. every day, excepting Sundays.

All visitors are respectfully requested to leave when the bell rings at the expiration of the visiting hour.

On Sundays visits to the patients are permitted only in cases of extreme sickness.

Officers of St. Luke's Hospital Association.

Right Rev. C. P. McIlvaine, D. D., *President.*

Right Rev. G. T. Bedell, D. D., *First Vice-President.*

Wm. Proctor,
T. G. Odiorne,　　　} *Vice-Presidents.*
Henry Probasco,

Managers.

William Proctor,
G. H. Barbour,
C. Wann,
Gideon Burton,
James A. Frazer,
G. K. Shoenberger,
Samuel Davis, Jr.,
D. B. Pierson,
T. G. Odiorne,
S. S. Rowe,
William Walter,
R. Wilson Lee,
Isaac C. Collins,
William M. Bush,
William B. Trott,
E. J. Miller,
B. Homans, Jr.,
H. Probasco,
John Cinnamon,
A. L. Frazer,
C. F. Bradley,
George H. Smith,
George T. Stedman,
H. D. Huntington,
W. J. M. Gordon,
John H. Hewson,
Wm. Henry Davis,
J. H. French,
William A. Proctor,
Seth L. Thompson,
H. B. Bissell,
Z. B. Coffin,
P. W. Strader.

BOARD OF COUNCIL AND ADVICE.

Right Rev. C. P. McIlvaine, D. D.
Right Rev. G. T. Bedell, D. D.

Rev. Richard Gray,
" J. H. Elliott,
" E. P. Wright,
" R. T. Kerfoot,
" Samuel Clements,
Rev. G. D. E. Mortimer,
" Francis Lobdell,
" Wm. Allen Fiske,
" Wm. A. Snively,
" D. H. Greer.

EXECUTIVE COMMITTEE.

T. G. Odiorne,   Wm. Henry Davis,
William Proctor,   G. H. Barbour,
John Cinnamon,   A. L. Frazer,
C. F. Bradley.

Wm. Henry Davis, *Treasurer.*
S. S. Rowe, *Secretary.*

AUDITING COMMITTEE.

C. F. Bradley,   Isaac C. Collins.

DAILY ATTENDING PHYSICIANS.

A. L. Carrick, M. D.   H. Ludington, M. D.
B. Taylor, M. D.   W. I. Wolfley, M. D.

CONSULTING PHYSICIANS.

C. G. Comegys, M. D.   Israel S. Dodge, M. D.
Geo. Mendenhall, M. D.   N. Foster, M. D.

ATTENDING SURGEONS.

P. S. Conner, M. D.   O. D. Norton, M. D.

CONSULTING SURGEONS.

Thomas Wood, M. D.   W. H. Mussey, M. D.

OCULIST.

E. Williams, M. D.

The attention of benevolent persons, who may be disposing of their property for charitable use, is directed to the following

FORM OF BEQUEST.

I give and bequeath to "St. Luke's Hospital Association of the Protestant Episcopal Church in the City of Cincinnati, Ohio," a Corporation created in the year 1865, under the laws of the State of Ohio, or to the Treasurer thereof, for the time being, for its corporate purposes, the sum of——dollars.

Dated at——.

FORM OF DEVISE OF REAL ESTATE.

I give and devise to "St. Luke's Hospital Association of the Protestant Episcopal Church in the City of Cincinnati, Ohio," a Corporation created in the year 1865, under the laws of the State of Ohio, or to the Treasurer thereof for the time being, for its corporate purposes, all that, etc. (here describe the property).

Dated at——.

WIDOWS' HOME.

This asylum for aged women was originated in 1848. After struggling through the first years of its existence, it became fixed in the public opinion as an object worthy of benevolence.

The charter was granted in 1851, the corporators being Robert Buchanan, Edward D. Mansfield, Davis B. Law-

ler, Lucius Brigham, Rufus King, Wesley Smead, John
Stille, and others. The establishment of the Home upon
a permanent footing, was largely owing to the personal
efforts of Wesley Smead, at that time a banker of the
city.

The following description of this institution is taken
from the valuable and interesting book, lately published, on the "Suburbs of Cincinnati."

"The object of the institution is to provide a home for
aged and indigent females, who can give satisfactory
testimonials of good conduct and respectable character.
Persons under sixty years of age are not admitted, though
this is not an invariable rule.

The fiscal affairs of the Home are under the control
of a Board of Trustees of three gentlemen, and the immediate management of all matters pertaining to the
household is reposed in a Board of Managers, consisting of twenty ladies. The present Matron is Mrs. M.
Oves, and the number of persons in the Home forty-
six.

The house is on the west side of Highland Avenue,
immediately opposite the German Protestant Orphan
Asylum. It consists of a large main three-story brick
edifice, facing the south, with wings of two stories on
both east and west, and a basement throughout the entire building. The house is airy, with good halls, comfortable well-furnished rooms, a parlor for the reception

11

of guests, and a room set apart for religious worship and other meetings. The location is an eligible one, and the surroundings desirable and pleasant.

The institution has an endowment fund, but this but partially defrays the current expenses. The benevolence of the community is looked to for the remainder.

The members of the family are compelled to do no more work than is desirable. Those who are able are expected to make their own beds and sweep their rooms each morning, to sew, knit, assist in domestic duties, and render all the service they can for the benefit of the institution and for those who are more helpless than themselves.

All that is necessary for their comfortable support is provided from the funds of the Society, and no person is allowed, under any circumstances, to leave the institution for assistance or work. Religious exercises are supplied by Rev. Joseph Emery, City Missionary, who preaches on alternate Wednesday afternoons. Services are also held by Rev. J. F. Wright, pastor of the Methodist Church in Mount Auburn; Rev. J. F. Lloyd, of High Street Church; Rev. J. Pierson, of Mears Chapel; and Rev. J. M. Straeffer. In addition to these, the students of Lane Seminary, during the session, hold regular Sabbath afternoon exercises."

This institution has done, and is doing, a noble work. Many aged, indigent women who, in better days, were surrounded by refinement and culture, have here been sheltered and cared for, and their declining days made brighter by the kindly offices of Christian benevolence.

The following regulations are observed:

1. No person shall be admitted into the asylum but those who bring satisfactory testimonials to the propriety of their conduct and the respectability of their character.

2. When they are pensioners on any church, benevolent institution, or society, it is expected their pensions will be continued, to assist in their support, and their funeral expenses will be defrayed.

3. No person under sixty years of age will be admitted; but the managers may, at their discretion, admit persons under that age, if satisfied that they have become helpless by premature old age.

4. Every person admitted as an inmate must pay a fee of one hundred dollars in advance.

5. No inmate who may be dismissed, or shall quit the asylum without the consent of the managers, will be re-admitted.

Officers.

Mrs. A. N. Riddle, *President.*
Mrs. John Shillito, *Vice-President.*
Mrs. Wm. Proctor, *Treasurer.*
Miss Clarissa Gest, *Secretary.*

Managers.

Mrs. A. E. Chamberlain,	Mrs. H. Thane Miller,
" R. Buchanan,	" Edw. Sargent,
" C. H. Stille,	" David James,
" J. P. Kilbreth,	" T. Maddox,
" Lawson,	" R. M. Corwine,
" G. D. Smith,	" G. H. Pendleton,
" J. Graff,	" McCormick,
" Thos. Butler,	" Benj. Bruce,
" Oliver Perin,	" Brooks Johnson,
" Eleanor Douglas,	" Theo. Cook.

Matron, Mrs. Oves.   *Assistant*, Mrs. Dryer.

Fiscal Trustees.

A. E. Chamberlain,   Edward Sargent,
W. W. Scarborough.

THE WOMEN'S CHRISTIAN ASSOCIATION

of Cincinnati was organized in June, 1868. The idea of its establishment originated with one of the most active members of the Young Men's Christian Association, a student of Lane Theological Seminary.

There had come under his attention the condition of the poorly-paid working girls of the city, and the thought was suggested to him of an organization that should do for young women what another association was already doing for young men.

After much deliberation and planning, the matter had at length become so well matured, that he deemed it time to take others into his counsels. Accordingly, he visited some two hundred ladies in the city, explained to them his views, showed the results he hoped to secure, met objections with convincing arguments, and at last won over to his views and side so many of the earnest Christian women of the city, that he thought a meeting might be safely called. So, one afternoon in the summer, after two months of hard preliminary work, in response to a call published in the papers, a small number of ladies assembled in the hall of the Y. M. C. A., for the purpose of forming a Women's Christian Association. Probably the hot weather kept some away; perhaps, too, the time was not yet fully ripe for the consummation of the work. At all events, after a little consultation, of a rather informal character, the meeting adjourned to meet again in the autumn. Early in October, invigorated by their summer wanderings, the ladies assembled once more.

Every one seemed to recognize the fact that the proposed institution, properly managed, would prevent the ultimate ruin of many a young stranger unused to the dangerous allurements of city life, and give a pleasant, cheerful home, at the mere cost of living, to others whose meager salaries would make such com-

forts otherwise impossible. The only wonder was, that
such a work had not long ago been undertaken. This
time all meant work, and before the meeting adjourned,
the movement had been inaugurated.

The plan that was adopted, looked, in the first place,
to the establishment of a boarding-house for women.
Of course, this is but a single direction of the many
in which the association proposes to work. Its scope
will be as comprehensive as that of the Young Men's
Association. But all the ladies seemed to feel that
more than any thing else there was needed a house
where young women, strangers in the city, either in
poorly-paid services, or in none at all, might find a
safe and comfortable home. So to the work of raising
funds for the leasing of a suitable building they at once
applied themselves.

Five thousand dollars were needed. This amount
was secured, and the association found itself upon a
firm basis of successful operation, with a host of good
friends and well-wishers.

A commodious building was leased, at No. 27 Longworth Street.

The churches were especially active in giving assistance. All denominations joined heartily in the work,
the Presbyterian shaking hands with the Swedenbor-
gian, the Baptist with the Unitarian, the Methodist
and Episcopalian with the Christian. The only rivalry

was to see which society should do most good with its money. Each church took upon itself the fitting up of a single room, aiming in its purchases to secure comfort. The result was, that the twenty-seven rooms in the building were provided neatly with black walnut furniture, oiled, with cheerful carpets, and other tasteful fittings. More attractive, cozy, comfortable rooms are hardly to be found in the city.

Upon the day of the opening of the Home, in March, 1869, these rooms were thronged. More than two thousand persons visited them, and the visitors were enthusiastic in their praise of the manner in which the work had been done.

In this, as in all large cities, there exists a class peculiarly needing sympathy and care. Attracted by the glitter of a city life, or seeking a livelihood for themselves, many young women leave quiet country homes, and flock to the crowded city. Far from home and protectors, inexperienced, friendless, and alone, they stand dismayed amid the perplexities, temptations, and wrongs of a great metropolis. They look in vain for a protecting hand and a sympathizing word. The common boarding-house is no place for them, and they can not pay half the prices demanded in those of a better class. At this point "Evil, with proffered hand and treacherous smile, stands ready to lead them on to ruin."

A prominent object of the institution is to furnish to such a temporary shelter. For these, the Home, with its welcome, comfort, and Christian influence, is open.

It is not to be thought of as a public institution, neither is it an ordinary boarding-house, where the lonely ones may live friendless and forgotten. It is a retired, pleasant home, the social and religious influences forming its chief characteristics.

A new and wide field of benevolence has thus been entered.

The Home will become the head-quarters of the great army of Christian women of the city. Bureaus will be organized, and new departments of Christian activity will be created. A field as broad as that occupied by the Young Men's Christian Association will be opened. A work as noble, as comprehensive, as vast, as important as the most tireless of workers could wish, will be afforded.

Officers.

Mrs. Dr. John Davis, *President.*

Vice-Presidents.

Mrs. S. S. Fisher,	Mrs. W. W. Scarborough,
" A. D. Bullock,	" J. F. Perry,
" Alphonso Taft,	" Dr. E. Williams.

Mrs. H. W. Sage, *Recording Secretary.*

"   Robert Brown, Jr., *Corresponding Secretary.*

Mrs. Dr. W. B. Davis, *Treasurer*.
Miss A. C. Crossette, *Auditor*.

Managers.

Mrs. D. W. Clark,
" A. F. Perry,
" B. F. Brannan,
" C. J. Acton,
" Jacob D. Cox,
" Thane Miller,
" Frank Whetstone,
" A. J. Howe,
" C. L. Thompson,

Mrs. George W. McAlpin,
" Elizabeth Dean,
" Murray Shipley,
" Mary J. Taylor,
" W. M. Bush,
Miss Mary Fitz,
" Hester Smith,
" Mary H. Sibley,
" Julia Carpenter.

YOUNG MEN'S CHRISTIAN ASSOCIATION.

The **Young Men's Christian** Association of Cincinnati deserves a high rank among the charities of the city. The suggestions of a wise and thoroughly earnest and practical Christianity are carried out in its present organization and methods of labor. The scope of these, and the means and ends of its usefulness, are well set forth in the following language:

"The Christian Association, in proportion to its membership and their activity, becomes a moral police wherever it is established, arresting the vicious in their mad career, preventing much of the sin that promises to ripen into crime, removing or diminishing, so far as its influence extends, the teeming temptations of city life, and attracting toward itself the confidence and love of those whose rescue has thus been wrought. By its well-arranged system of practical fraternity, the institution provides employment for the unemployed, homes and churches and friends for the stranger, nurses and physicians for the sick, and all this without other incentive than the consciousness of discharging duty and the hope of winning souls to Christ. It makes not membership the sole title to its benefits, it exacts no oaths of secrecy, it assumes no prerogatives of power or privilege, it puts forth no pretension to peculiar sanctity."

On the evening of the 8th of October, 1848, a band of young men organized, in Cincinnati, a "society for mutual improvement in grace and religious knowledge." At first, the Central Presbyterian Church only was represented, but, three months later, January 8, 1849, they had discovered a ready sympathy with their objects on the part of others, and the organization was extended to all denominations, founded on the broad principle of Christian union.

Its meetings, with a view to mental and spiritual improvement, were occupied by reports of the members from mission fields at a distance, of home work among the churches of the city, and of personal experience, especially in labors with young men whom they sought to bring in—if Christians, to work with them; if not

Christians, that they might do them good. A special membership was provided identical with the present "Associate Membership." Later, in 1850, a "Contributing Membership" was formed.

The society was designated, early in its history, as the "Young Men's Society of Inquiry;" later, April, 1849, as the "Cincinnati Society of Religious Inquiry;" then, in the spring of 1853, when the existence of similar organizations had become known and sympathies had been exchanged, the addition to the title of "Young Men's Christian Union" was made; and, in 1858, the latter title was used exclusively. In May, 1863, the name "Young Men's Christian Association" was adopted to secure uniformity in title with the kindred organizations which had now been formed in every section of the country.

The early progress of the Cincinnati society had been gradual but sure. It became a power in the community known and felt by a large number, especially of young men. Its life was quickened when, in 1853, it learned of other societies which had been established with identically the same objects, at London, in June, 1844; at Montreal, December, 1851; and at Boston, December 29, 1851. The societies at London and Cincinnati were entirely independent of, and unknown to, each other until about this time. In 1853, the number of associations had increased to twenty-five.

Thus, the cause had come to be a power in the whole land, and with its growth each society grew. A confederation was formed of nearly all the associations on the continent in 1855, and from that time the institution began to assume larger proportions, and greater uniformity and wisdom of purpose.

The Cincinnati association pursued its work with success till 1861. The breaking out of the civil war then interfered seriously with its operations, and, for two or three years, it practically ceased to exist.

On the 18th of July, 1865, the present society, in full sympathy with the former organization, adopted a constitution, which, as amended May 7, 1867, is now in force.

The first meetings were held in the lecture room of the Seventh Street Congregational Church, until a room was procured at No. 54 West Fourth Street.

The accommodations here being insufficient, new quarters were sought. The present premises of the Association, at 200 and 202 Vine Street, were first occupied in September, 1865. At this time, William J. Breed was President. His administration was marked with vigor and unprecedented success, and the institution took rank among the leading forces arrayed against the vice, pauperism, and crime of the great city. In 1868, H. Thane Miller was elected President, and the Association has received a new impetus in its glorious work. It has

felt in its every department the earnest spirit and en-
thusiasm of such a leader.

The object of the Association is to promote the mental, moral, and spiritual welfare of the young men of
Cincinnati.

The plan has been to divide the work into departments, each under the care of an efficient committee,
and to have the whole field under the supervision of
an executive board. Reports from all committees are
made in writing, once a month, and are read at the
business meeting of the Association.

THE READING ROOM is free to all. It has been constantly open from eight A. M. to ten P. M., and has
been a pleasant resort for thousands of homeless young
men.

THE MUSIC ROOM adjoins the reading room, and is
made as homelike as possible, with pictures and illu-
minated texts on the walls, a piano, cabinet organ, and
other attractions. This is designed for the large class
of homeless young men who wander up and down the
streets, cheerless and forlorn, and who, because they are
homeless, are so easily beguiled into the gilded haunts
of vice and infamy. In this room they meet pleasaut
faces, a smile of welcome, and a cordial grasp of the
hand.

Social meetings are held on the third Tuesday evening of the month, to which ladies and gentlemen are

cordially invited.   Readings, recitations, music, and conversation fill the evening.

THE CONVERSATION ROOM is open every evening, and has been visited by not less than twenty thousand young men during the year. As many as three hundred and fifty have been present in a single evening. All enjoy the innocent games, and as soon as they cross the threshold realize the necessity of gentlemanly language and deportment. This room has kept many young men from scenes of dissipation, and has proved the starting point toward a better life.

A lyceum has been established, under the auspices of the Association, and weekly meetings are held. Essays, debates, and criticisms occupy the evening.

Missionary work has been carried on most successfully. There are many institutions of relief, punishment, and reform, with every attention paid to the physical wants of the inmates, but no adequate provision made for their spiritual wants. A committee was appointed to supervise the field, and volunteers came forward to visit the jail, the city prison, the work-house, hospitals, and other public institutions, on the Sabbath. Religious tracts and papers were distributed, personal conversations were held with the patients and prisoners, and religious services conducted in the wards and chapels.

A Bible class, conducted by clergymen and laymen alternately, is held every Sunday. A noonday religious service has been regularly sustained, and one or more evening prayer meetings every week. On the Sabbath, the Gospel has been proclaimed at every possible point specially adapted to collect an audience of non-church-goers; parks, market-spaces, theaters, and public halls have been turned into places of prayer.

THE STRANGER'S HOME, open during the cold season, proved a great benefaction to hundreds of homeless wanderers. A building was engaged with sufficient space for a large kitchen, dining room, and dormitories; charitable persons, in different parts of the city, purchased tickets, and, when needy persons applied to them for assistance, tickets were given, with directions where to find the "Stranger's Home." Tickets can not be converted into money, nor spent for liquor. More than one hundred men frequently slept there at night who would otherwise have been inmates of the station-houses. In the daytime they were provided with plain, wholesome food, and with bathing facilities. Cleanly habits were strictly enjoined, good order preserved, good morals taught.

COFFEE ROOM.—It is nearly three years since the Workingmen's Coffee and Reading Room was opened on the corner of John and Columbia Streets. It speedily became self-supporting, and has proved of great benefit to the class for whom it was specially designed. The aim was to furnish coffee and soup as substitutes for beer and stronger drinks, at a price so cheap that men would come from motives of economy. The plan was successful.

The drinking saloons in the vicinity have lost customers, and in four instances have suspended operations entirely.

An employment register is kept, looking to the relief of young men by finding for them situations. Hundreds of young men every year receive temporary assistance in the way of shelter, food, clothing, or transportation to distant homes. Friendless strangers, in hotels and boarding-houses, are cared for in sickness and death. Thus widely is this glorious institution stretching the arms of its usefulness. Its achievements shall be unmeasured in time, and its far-reaching results known only in eternity.

Officers of the Association.

H. Thane Miller, *Prest.* R. S. Fulton, *Rec. Secy.*
W. J. Breed, *Vice-Prest.* John H. Cheever, *Treas.*
H. P. Lloyd, *Cor. Secy.* L. Sheaff, *Superintendent.*

Executive Committee.

H. Thane Miller, H. P. Clough,
W. J. Breed, W. R. Kidd,
H. P. Lloyd, Cyrus S. Bates,
R. S. Fulton, L. R. Hull,
J. H. Cheever, Abner L. Frazer,

Lang Sheaff.

Finance Committee.

S. J. Broadwell,	Hugh McBirney,
B. Homans, Jr.,	W. H. Doane,
James B. Wilson,	H. W. Brown,
W. F. Thorne,	W. J. Breed,
Matthew Addy,	Theo. Cook,

C. W. Starbuck.

Standing Committees.

RECEPTION.

Jas. C. McCurdy,	Chas. E. Hayward,

C. E. Wood.

PRAYER MEETING.

Wm. G. McL. Doering,	John L. Ledman,

Mr. Springit.

BIBLE CLASS.

Walter Alden,	L. H. Swormstedt.

SABBATH EVENING SERVICES.

S. M. Chester,	W. H. Davis.

THEATER SERVICES.

S. Lowry,	Geo. E. Stevens,

J. A. Grover.

12

HOSPITALS.

G. H. Smith, T. B. Horton,
Jos. Riggs.

COUNTY JAIL.

John Stuyvesant, E. M. Crevath,
W. J. Baker, Jr.

U. S. BARRACKS.

B. F. Barry, S. B. Brown,
Walter Tearne.

WORK-HOUSE.

C. Hitchcock, L. Parker,
H. J. Page, H. P. Hopkins.

FEMALE PRISON.

George Gray, D. I. Jones.

LYCEUM.

E. H. Foster.

LECTURES.

Sidney D. Maxwell, S. L. Frazer,
H. M. Taylor.

SOCIAL MEETINGS.

J. F. Crossett, T. M. Hinkle,
E. G. Hall.

HOUSE OF REFUGE CINCINNATI

STRANGERS HOME.

J. Emery, W. S. How,
Wm. B. Williamson.

EMPLOYMENT.

R. A. Holden, E. S. Lloyd,
C. S. Morten.

BOARDING HOUSES.

C. A. Aiken, H. Griggs,
W. C. Herron.

COFFEE ROOMS.

Murray Shipley, W. E. London,
S. C. Tatem.

LIBRARY AND PERIODICALS.

J. T. Perry, R. D. Barney,
H. P. B. Jewett.

COLORED ORPHAN ASYLUM.

This institution aims to accomplish for colored children the ends contemplated in kindred organizations. Its building is at Avondale. Statistics of its operations are not at hand.

CINCINNATI HOUSE OF REFUGE.

This institution was established in 1850. Its support is provided for by law, although its operations enlist the sympathies of many who manifest their interest by substantial tokens of regard.   In the magnitude of its work and the great good accomplished by it, it yields to no other institution.   It stands a monument to the memory of the philanthropic citizens who urged its necessity, and saw after many years the consummation of their noble endeavors.   Prominent among these gentlemen were William Burnet, Thomas J. Biggs, George Crawford, H. B. Curtis, Miles Greenwood, E. P. Langdon, William McCammon, Joseph Ray, Alphonso Taft, and Charles Thomas.

The object of the institution is the reformation of depraved and unmanageable children in the city of Cincinnati.   The majority are sent here from the Police Court.   In September, 1868, there were inmates one hundred and sixty boys and thirty-four girls.   Their mental and moral training is of the best character, and a large number learn to excel in mechanical employments.   This labor, besides its reformatory influence, is a source of considerable income.   Many leave the walls of this institution to rise rapidly in the social scale, and take their places as useful members of society.

Under the superintendence of H. A. Monfort, Esq., the House of Refuge is fulfilling the most sanguine hopes of its founders.   No institution of its kind in the United States is better managed.

The buildings are situated in Millcreek Valley, one

mile north of corporation line. The buildings are of blue limestone, with windows, cornices, casings, and portico of white Dayton stone, and are erected in the Grecian style. The grounds belonging to the institution contain nine and seven-eighths acres, five and three-fourths of which are inclosed by a stone wall twenty feet high, within which stand all the buildings except the stable.

The "House" presents an imposing front of two hundred and seventy-seven feet, and is composed of a main building, eighty-five by fifty-five feet, four stories in height, with towers at the extremities projecting two feet in front, and which are five stories high, besides the basement. In the main building are the offices, superintendents' and officers' apartment, principal store-room, boys' hospitals and dispensary.

Extending north and south from the main building are two wings, each ninety-six by thirty-eight, with towers at the extremities projecting two feet in front and rear. The wings are four stories in height, and the towers five, besides the basement. The buildings will accommodate three hundred and fifty inmates, with the requisite officers.

Board of Directors.

A. E. Chamberlain,	Jos. C. Butler,
Charles Thomas,	R. A. Holden,

Chas. F. Wilstach,   H. Thane Miller,
S. Bonner,   Jas. M. Johnston,
John D. Minor.

Officers.

A. E. Chamberlain, *President.*
Joseph C. Butler, *Treasurer.*
H. A. Monfort, *Superintendent and Secretary.*
A. B. Chase, *Assistant Superintendent.*

Joseph Chester, *Chaplain.*
Mrs. M. Fleckinger, *Matron.*
Miss S. G. Paulson, *Nurse.*
Mrs. E. Wilson, *Housekeeper.*
W. H. Taylor, *Acting Physician.*
G. F. Magaw,
Wm. Wilcox,   } *Teachers.*
Mrs. E. M. Herrick,
Miss Auretta Hoyt,

BOARD OF HEALTH.

The Board of Health was established in 1867, and has accomplished most desirable results. The Mayor of the city is President, *ex-officio.*

John F. Torrence, *President.*
William Clendenin, M. D., *Health Officer.*
Guy W. Armstrong, *Secretary.*

Hugh McBirney,	S. S. Davis,
Charles Thomas,	John Simpkinson,
J. C. Baum,	John Hauck.

THE CITY INFIRMARY

is a municipal institution, affording relief in the shape of coal, tickets to the Soup House, and admission into the City Infirmary. The office is on Plum Street, between Seventh and Eighth. The buildings of the Infirmary are located on the Carthage road, eight and a half miles north of the city. The farm contains one hundred and sixty acres of beautifully rolling land. The spacious edifice, recently erected, is an ornament to its vicinity, and the position commands a fine view of the surrounding country.

Application for relief must be made to the overseers of the poor.

The Directors of the City Infirmary are Messrs. W. H. Watters, Ira Wood, and John Martin.

LONGVIEW ASYLUM.

This institution for the treatment of lunatics is described elsewhere. Its Board of Directors are—

Judge John Burgoyne, *President.*
Hon. Joshua H. Bates, *Secretary.*

Hon. Jno. F. Torrence,	Hon. Henry Kessler,
Joseph Siefert, Esq.,	Hon. John K. Green.

It has the following corps of officers:

O. M. Langdon, M. D., *Supt. and Physician.*
A. P. Courtwright, M. D., *Assistant Physician.*
R. T. Thorburn, Esq., *Steward.*
Mrs. Louisa W. Jones, *Matron.*

THE CINCINNATI HOSPITAL.

The object of this institution is to provide medical attendance for the sick poor of Cincinnati. Patients who are able to pay and non-residents incur a charge of five dollars per week for board, medicines, and treatment. The advancement of medical science is consulted in the provision of clinical lectures, to which all medical students who have regularly matriculated in a medical college may be admitted.

The government and control of the hospital is vested in a board of seven trustees, of which the Mayor of the city and the director of the City Infirmary, oldest in commission, are members *ex-officio.* One trustee is appointed by the Governor of the State, two by the Superior Court, and two by the Court of Common Pleas. The present board are—

Hon. John F. Torrence, *President.*
J. J. Quinn, M. D., *Secretary.*

B. F. Brannan, Esq.,	David Judkins, M. D.,
F. J. Mayer, Esq.,	John Carlisle, Esq.,

Ira Wood, Esq.

Henry M. Jones, *Superintendent.*
T. E. H. McLean, *Clerk.*
Agnes Rose, *Matron.*
Charles Biele, *Druggist.*

PHYSICIANS.

C. G. Comegys, M. D.,   John A. Murphy, M. D.,
John Davis, M. D.,   J. F. White, M. D.

SURGEONS.

W. H. Mussey, M. D.,   W. W. Dawson, M. D.,
H. E. Foote, M. D.,   Wm. Clendenin, M. D.

OBSTETRICIANS.

M. B. Wright, M. D.,   Geo. Mendenhall, M. D.

OCULISTS.

E. Williams, M. D.,   W. W. Seeley, M. D.

PATHOLOGISTS.

W. H. Taylor, M. D.,   Roberts Bartholow, M. D.,
Wm. Carson, M. D.

PHYSICIAN TO PEST-HOUSE.

J. L. Neilson, M. D.

CHIEF HOUSE PHYSICIANS.

J. L. Quinn, M. D.,   Jas. Dawson, M. D.,
J. B. Richie, M. D.

ASSISTANT HOUSE PHYSICIANS.

S. W. Anderson, M. D.,   H. Illowy, M. D.,
W. W. Vinnedge, M. D.

This summary view is, of course, too limited to present a statement of all public charitable efforts in a city of the size of Cincinnati. No mention has been made of the widely-extended benevolent operations of the Masonic and other secret organizations, and the various trades' unions, through whose agencies large sums are spent in the alleviation of human suffering. The vast system of the Roman Catholics, who, within the archdiocese of Cincinnati, have two orphan asylums, two hospitals, and six charitable institutions of different kinds; the extensive efforts made within the bounds of the Episcopal Church and other Protestant denominations, and other special methods, remain without full statistics or extended notice. Ample evidence has been given, however, that benevolent effort is wide-awake and effective in this great metropolis, and that, in this golden age of Charity, the Queen City may compare its record with any.

CHAPTER VII.

CINCINNATI may justly boast of the excellent
quality and high tone of its daily press. Nowhere
in the land, outside of New York, are newspapers
conducted upon an equal scale of expense. The journals of the Queen City challenge comparison the world
over for beauty of typography and value of contents;
while, as mediums of reaching the public, they rank
higher with advertisers than those of any other city,
New York alone excepted.

The Commercial is published in the quarto form, is
independent in politics, and claims the largest circulation in the Mississippi Valley. No expense is spared
in its service of the public, and it has performed most
astonishing feats in giving the earliest publicity to important news. It keeps an impartial and sleepless eye
upon current affairs. *The Commercial* is published by
M. Halstead & Co., and is issued every morning in the
week.

The Chronicle, an evening paper, is in the second year of its existence, and full of the energy and sprightliness of a vigorous youth. In the presentation of literary and scientific intelligence, with its general news, it is unsurpassed. The public spirit and sagacity of its publishers have entitled them to the remarkable success they have achieved. *The Chronicle* is Republican in politics.

The Enquirer, the Democratic organ, is one of the best conducted newspapers in the country. Liberal in spirit and enterprising in management, it wields enormous power throughout the South and West. Its conductors, Messrs. Faran & McLean, thoroughly understand the art of journalism, and produce a paper which may safely invite comparison.

The Gazette, Republican in politics, is now in the fifty-second year of its existence, and in the full tide of prosperity. Its various departments enlist first-class talent, and its influence in the formation of public opinion is immense. As a business newspaper it is invaluable, its columns embodying all current facts and documents of commercial interest. Matter of permanent historical value which is constantly appearing, makes it most valuable for preservation.

The Times, published in the evening, is the oldest daily in Cincinnati with one exception, having been established in 1840. Its columns give evidence of unceasing care and vigilance in the publication of all matters of general public interest. Independent of party, it seeks to fill all the requirements of a newspaper for the family circle. Its weekly edition has a circulation of nearly seventy thousand, and goes into every State and Territory in the Union.

To meet the wants of the large German citizenship, two dailies are published in the German language, every morning.

The Volksblatt, Republican in politics, is published by Hof & Hassaurek.

The Volksfreund, of the Democratic persuasion, is published by a stock company.

Each of the morning papers publish weekly editions.

The other papers and periodicals published in the city are here given:

WEEKLIES.

American Christian Review (Christian). Published by Franklin & Rice. Circulation, 9,500.

Catholic Telegraph.

Christian Apologist (German Methodist). Circulation, 16,000. Published by Hitchcock & Walden.

Christian Herald (New School Presbyterian). Circulation, 8,000.

Christian World (Reformed Church). Circulation, 5,000.

Cincinnati Price Current. William Smith, Editor and Proprietor.

Cincinnati Wahrheitsfreund (German Catholic). Circulation, 14,000.

Free Nation. Published by Amos Moore.

Journal and Messenger (Baptist). Circulation, 5,500.

Literary Eclectic. Published by H. M. Moos.

Presbyter (Old School Presbyterian). Circulation, 5,200. Published by Monfort & Wampler.

Protestantische Zeitblatter. Published by Edw. Luther.

Railroad Record. Published by Wrightson & Co.

Temperance Age. John Gundry, Editor and Proprietor.

Sendbote (German Baptist). Circulation, 3,000. Rev. P. W. Bickel, Editor.

The Deborah. Published by Bloch & Co.

The Israelite. Published by Bloch & Co.

The Star in the West (Universalist). Circulation, 5,300. Published by Williamson & Cantwell.

Western Christian Advocate (Methodist). Circulation, 25,000. Published by Hitchcock & Walden.

SEMI-MONTHLY.

Sunday School Advocate (Methodist).

Sunday School Bell (German Methodist). Rev. W. Nast, D. D., Editor.

MONTHLY.

Children's Home Record. Rev. B. W. Chidlaw, Editor.

Christian Press. Circulation, 23,000. Rev. B. P. Aydelott, D. D., Editor.

Christian Pulpit. Rev. N. Summerbell, D. D., Editor.

Dental Register. Dr. J. Taft, Editor.

Eclectic Medical Journal. J. M. Scudder, M. D., Editor.

Family Treasure. Rev. Jos. Chester, Editor.

Journal of Medicine. George C. Blackman, M. D., Editor.

Ladies' Repository. Circulation, 34,000. Rev. I. W. Wiley, D. D., Editor.

Lancet and Observer. Dr. E. B. Stevens, Publisher.

Medical Repository. J. A. Thacker, M. D., Editor.

Masonic Review. Cornelius Moore, Editor.

National Normal. R. H. Holbrook, Editor.

Phonographic Magazine. Benn Pitman, Publisher.

Painter's Magazine.

Sabbath School Missionary. Circulation, 22,000. Western Tract & Book Society.

Sæmann (German Baptist). Circulation, 10,000.

Sabbath Paper. Circulation, 12,000. Western Tract & Book Society.

The Treasury (Welsh). Charles Bathgate, Editor.

The Theological Eclectic. Moore, Wilstach & Moore, Publishers.

Temperance Review. John Moffatt, Editor.

QUARTERLY.

The Christian Quarterly.   Rev. W. T. Moore, Editor

Cincinnati, with its numerous newspapers and periodicals, produces also, largely, literature of a more permanent character, ranking fourth among American cities in the manufacture of books. An immense capital is embarked in the publishing business. Messrs. Wilson, Hinkle & Co., publish a series of text-books, of which over three million copies are sold annually. It is the largest publishing house of elementary school books in the world. The Methodist Book Concern publish over twenty-five hundred separate volumes, and turn out, under the supervision of the veteran printer, R. P. Thompson, work which can challenge comparison with the finest printing done in the Atlantic cities. The Elm Street Printing Company, besides other business, print more than twenty different periodicals, which distribute to the public annually over fifty million pages of reading matter.

THE CINCINNATI CHAMBER OF COMMERCE.

This organization, which has attained such influence and prominence in its relations to the commerce of the United States, was established in 1839. The following board of officers was elected January 14, 1840:

Griffin Taylor, *President.*

Vice-Presidents.

R. G. Mitchell,	Thomas J. Adams,
John Reeves,	S. B. Findley,
Peter Neff,	Samuel Trevor.

B. W. Hewson, *Treasurer.*
Henry Rockey, *Secretary.*

Subsequent **Presidents** have been Lewis Whiteman, R. G. Mitchell, **Thomas J. Adams**, James C. Hall, N. W. Thomas, **R. M. W. Taylor**, James F. Torrence, Joseph Torrence, J. W. Sibley, Jos. C. Butler, George F. Davis, Theodore Cook, S. C. Newton, and John A. Gano.

The object in view was to afford occasion and place for the discussion of all leading questions of mercantile usage, of matters of finance, and of laws affecting commerce, **and** also to collect information in relation to commercial, financial, and industrial affairs that might be of general interest and value; to secure uniformity in commercial laws and customs; to facilitate business intercourse **and to promote equitable principles, as well** as the adjustment of differences and disputes in trade.

OFFICERS OF THE CHAMBER OF COMMERCE.

President.
John A. Gano.

Vice-Presidents.

J. H. French,	H. M. Johnston,
A. L. Frazer,	Wm. Henry Davis,
S. F. Covington,	Florence Marmet.

William Shaffer, *Treasurer.*
George McLaughlin, *Secretary.*
William Smith, *Sup't Merchants Exchange.*

THE BOARD OF TRADE OF CINCINNATI.

This organization was formed in 1868, to represent and promote the immense industrial interests which make Cincinnati the third in importance of manufacturing cities in the United States. Its effort will be to collect and record such local and general statistical information relating to manufactures and commerce as may promote the manufacturing, commercial, and financial welfare of the city of Cincinnati, and especially to protect, foster, and develop its manufacturing and industrial interests.

Any person, a resident of Cincinnati, or of Hamilton County, State of Ohio, or of Campbell or Kenton Counties, State of Kentucky, or any firm or corporation doing business within said limits, if approved by the Executive Board of Officers, may become an active member of this association upon payment of the annual dues prescribed.

Executive Board.

Miles Greenwood, *President.*
Robert Mitchell, *First Vice-President.*
A. T. Goshorn, *Second Vice-President.*
S. S. Davis, *Treasurer.*

Trustees.

Joseph Kinsey,   M. Kleiner,
James L. Haven,   Josiah Kirby,
        A. P. C. Bonte.
        H. H. Tatem, *Secretary.*

LIBRARIES.

The Public Library is under the direction of a
Board of Managers chosen by the Board of Education.
This Board of Managers is now as follows:

J. M. Walden, *Chairman.*   J. B. Powell, *Sec'y.*
        M. D. Hanover, *Treasurer.*

Rufus King,   Robert Brown, Jr.,
H. Eckel,   S. S. Fisher.

The number of volumes in the library is 23,786. Of
these, 16,196 volumes belong to the Public Library,
5,852 volumes to the Ohio Mechanics Institute, and
1,738 volumes to the Historical Society of Ohio. This
extensive collection is for the free use of all residents
of the city. It is constantly growing, and in time will

occupy a new building which, in convenience of arrangement, will be surpassed by none in the land.

YOUNG MEN'S MERCANTILE LIBRARY.

This institution was established in 1835. Moses Ranney was the first President. Its members now number 2,141. The library contains 30,499 volumes.

The library and reading rooms are handsomely fitted up and are well stocked with books in every department of general literature, and newspapers and periodicals from all parts. There is no more pleasant resort than these rooms, in the College building on Walnut Street, above Fourth.

Officers.

Frank H. Baldwin, *President.*
Albert W. Mullen, *Vice-President.*
W. R. Looker, *Corresponding Secretary.*
Charles B. Murray, *Recording Secretary.*
Hugh Colville, *Treasurer.*

Directors.

James M. Clark, Samuel McKeehan,
John J. Rickey, Alexander Clark,
William T. Tibbitts.

M. Hazen White, A. M., *Librarian and Sup't.*
W. E. Barnwell, A. B., *First Assistant.*
A. McLean, *Second Assistant.*

GENERAL THEOLOGICAL AND RELIGIOUS LIBRARY.

The association controlling this collection was formed in 1864. Its object is to form a complete collection of religious literature, representing every creed and every shade of theological belief. An apartment in the edifice of the Mechanics Institute, on the corner of Sixth and Vine, is occupied at present. The library comprises 3,800 volumes.

THE LAW LIBRARY,

one of the best in the country, is alluded to elsewhere.

The above embraces the principal collections in the city, though there are many others of minor importance.

The limits of this volume will not suffice to mention, at length, the various associations, literary, scientific, social, and otherwise, which exist in Cincinnati, and give tone to public opinion and means of social improvement. A few of these will, however, be noticed.

CINCINNATI HORTICULTURAL SOCIETY.

This society was organized in 1843, Robert Buchanan being one of the most active of its originators. Its career has been a prosperous one, and its influence has been felt far and wide in the promotion of knowledge and achievements in the growth of fruits and flowers.

Exhibitions are held semi-annually. The President
of the Society is W. P. Anderson, Esq.

ACADEMY OF MEDICINE.

This organization, formed in 1867, meets weekly, for
the discussion of appropriate subjects, and for other
objects of special interest to the medical profession.
W. W. Dawson, M. D., is President.

THE HISTORICAL AND PHILOSOPHICAL SOCIETY

was organized in 1824, and has been of great value in
preserving facts relative to the history of the West,
and in subserving the interests of science and literature generally. Robert Buchanan is its President.

THE OHIO MECHANICS INSTITUTE

was incorporated in 1829. It provides, annually, at
a mere nominal cost, the best instruction in practical
branches of knowledge for any who choose to partake
of its benefits.

THE PIONEERS ASSOCIATION

is composed of the early settlers and those born here
previous to July 4, 1812. It was organized in 1856,
and celebrates, each year, the settlement of Ohio, upon
the 6th of April, and the settlement of Cincinnati,
upon the 26th of December. Thomas H. Yeatman is
its President.

THE YOUNG MENS' GYMNASTIC ASSOCIATION

is alluded to elsewhere in this volume.

THE GERMAN PIONEER ASSOCIATION

was organized in 1868, and now numbers about three
hundred members. It publishes a monthly periodical,
which will embody much valuable information in regard
to pioneer history. Through the kindness of the officers
of the society, the engraving of Cincinnati in 1802 has
been furnished.

LANE SEMINARY

has long been a prominent institution of Cincinnati. Its
early history made it known and famous throughout the
country, associating with it the names of Rev. Dr. Ly-
man Beecher, Rev. Dr. Thomas Biggs, Rev. Calvin E.
Stowe, and others. Situated at Walnut Hills, it has
made that locality marked as the point whence have
gone forth hundreds of ministers who are now laboring
in every quarter of the globe. The library is one of
the best in the United States, containing about fifteen
thousand volumes.

The present faculty consists of Rev. D. Howe Allen,
Emeritus Professor of Systematic Theology; Rev. Henry
Smith, Professor of Sacred Rhetoric and Biblical Literature; Rev. Henry A. Nelson, Professor of Systematic
and Pastoral Theology; Rev. Edward D. Morris, Pro-

fessor of Ecclesiastical History and Church Polity, and Rev. Llewelyn J. Evans, Professor of Hebrew and Greek Exegesis.

Cincinnati may be proud of its provisions for the education of females. Among the many institutions of this kind may be mentioned the Wesleyan Female College, which is described elsewhere. Professor Lucius H. Bugbee is now the President. Professor C. C. Bragdon occupies the chair of ancient languages.

THE MOUNT AUBURN YOUNG LADIES' INSTITUTE,

established in 1856, has always held the first rank as a school of thorough culture and the best advantages. Its admirable location and facilities for its work continue to attract to it a large number of pupils. Rev. A. J. Rowland is at the head of this institution.

THE CINCINNATI LITERARY CLUB,

John W. Herron, President; John M. Newton, Secretary, is well sustained. Besides this, there are the Burns, Davenport, Old Woodward, Shakspeare, St. Elmo, U. C. D. and Yale Clubs, all with hosts of friends, and enjoying a vigorous life. The association of German Turners wields great influence. The Allemania, Caledonia, and St. George Societies are well-known organizations.

THOS SHERLOCK, Prest
JOHN W. HARTWELL, Vice Prest
R. E. LEE, Secretary.
WM F. CHURCH, Adjuster
J. DeW. CHURCHILL, Supervisor.
Enterprise Insurance Co.
CAPITAL $1,000,000.
Cincinnati,
SEE BUILDING, PAGE 203.

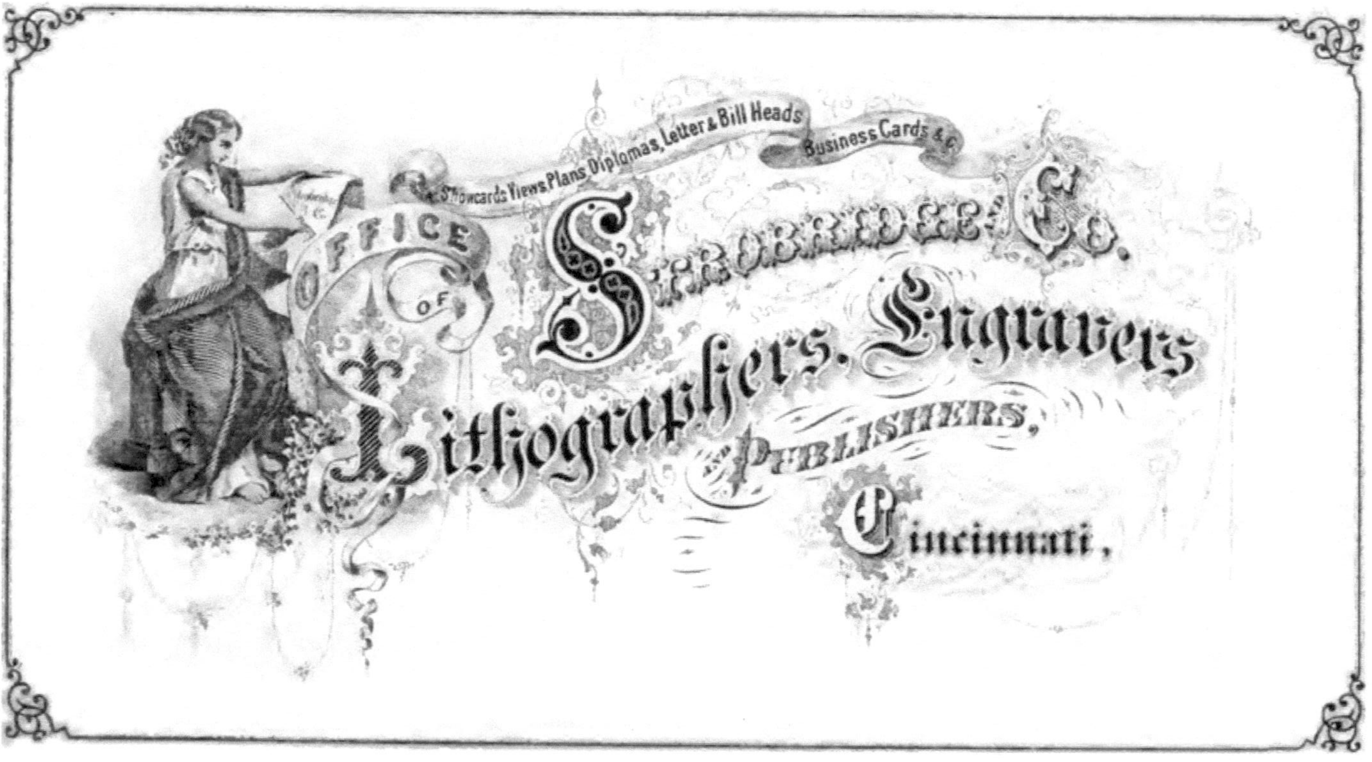
Showcards Views Plans Diplomas, Letter & Bill Heads Business Cards &c
OFFICE OF
STROBRIDGE & CO.
Lithographers, Engravers
AND PUBLISHERS,
Cincinnati,

The Männerchor, the Harmonic, Cecilia and other musical societies, which are amply supported, give evidence of cultivation and taste in the divine art.

This hasty survey will give but a glimpse at the social elements of Cincinnati. There is a high social, intellectual, and religious tone, and true public spirit. Its private collections of literature and art are famous, and in all that aids and adorns civilization, this great metropolis need not fear comparison with older American cities.

CHAPTER VIII.

ITEMS OF CAUTION AND NOTICE—HORSE-CAR ROUTES—FIRE-ALARM STATIONS—LINES OF OUTWARD TRAVEL—MISCELLANEOUS.

THE stranger in any large city may avail himself of facilities which will soon make him entirely at home, and almost independent of the vague information to be obtained by asking questions. In Cincinnati, Williams & Co.'s Directory, prepared with great accuracy, and to be found at every hotel, will give almost all items of knowledge desired by the visitor.

No more than a word is needed here to caution persons against being imposed upon by the various "confidence games" which have been so often exposed. Pickpockets are emphatically a city "institution," and wherever there is a crowd, it is well to beware of them. Money should never be shown among strangers, and large sums should always be deposited in bank, or in other trustworthy hands.

All the banks and express offices require identification of persons drawing money or obtaining goods.

SOUTH-WEST CORNER OF

Race & Pearl Sts.

To our Friends and the Public:

Having removed to our *splendid new five-story stone-front buildings,
Nos. 85 and 87 Race Street*, two doors south of the corner of Race and
Pearl Streets, we take great pleasure in announcing to our numerous
customers and friends, that we enter these new buildings with *increased facilities every way* for furnishing a large and well-selected stock
of Groceries at the *very lowest prices*. Mr. R. M. Bishop, the senior
member of the firm, who will give his personal attention, as heretofore, to purchasing for the house, has had forty years' experience as
a merchant, and twenty-two years of that time in the

Wholesale Grocery Business,

in this city, and we feel assured that he *can and will* buy our stock at
such advantages as will enable us to sell at lower rates than houses
that have not our experience or our facilities.

As the reputation of our house is so well established, we do not
think it necessary to send solicitors or drummers through the country, but prefer to give our customers the advantage of this very considerable expense, and *we will do it* with all who may send us their
orders. *All we ask is to give us a fair trial*, and we feel confident that we
will be able to give entire satisfaction.

Our stock of

TEAS, TOBACCOS, AND CIGARS

will always be found *large and complete*—selected with great care and
purchased from first hands. This branch of our business will be
under the special charge of one of the firm, and we feel confident we
can offer inducements in these articles.

Call and see us at our New Stores, Nos. 85 & 87 Race Street,

and you will always receive a cordial welcome; but, if not convenient
to visit the city, *send us your orders*, and you can rely upon their being
promptly and satisfactorily filled.

Respectfully,

R. M. BISHOP & CO.,
85 and 87 Race Street.

Geo. S. Blanchard & Co.,

Publishers, Booksellers, and Stationers,

CINCINNATI,

Call attention to their well-assorted stock of Books and Stationery. Their established reputation and long experience guarantee faithful and intelligent dealing with their customers. Book-buyers will find upon their shelves a select stock of Standard works in every department of Literature. History, Poetry, Science, Fiction, Belles-Lettres, etc., are well represented. All New Publications are promptly received. Parties residing at a distance from the city will find it very much to their advantage to correspond with G. S. B. & Co., in reference to whatever they may wish in their line. Particular attention is given to supplying College, Society, and Private Libraries. To Purchasers for Libraries, Professional Men, Teachers, and Students, liberal terms are offered. Every variety of Stationery, Blank Books, Writing Papers, and Envelopes will be furnished at the lowest rates.

The Public are requested to call and examine our stock; or, if unable to visit Cincinnati, to communicate with us by Letter. All orders will receive prompt attention, and information of the prices at which articles can be furnished will be cheerfully given.

GEO. S. BLANCHARD & CO.,

No. 39 West Fourth St., Cincinnati.

MESSRS. GEO. S. BLANCHARD & Co. will publish, in May, 1869, a volume descriptive of the

SUBURBS OF CINCINNATI.

"No inland city in the world surpasses Cincinnati in the beauty of its environs."—ATLANTIC MONTHLY.

The work will embrace a historical sketch of each of the principal suburban localities and detailed descriptions of the various attractions and beauties which have given the environs of Cincinnati a wide celebrity. It will possess great interest for every resident of the city and every tourist who visits the "Queen of the West."

Frederik Schultze
Stephan Wagner
F. SCHULTZE & Co.
IMPORTERS & DEALERS IN
PARIAN MARBLE,
LAVA
AND
FANCY GOODS.
CHINA,
GLASS
AND
QUEENSWARE.
No 73
West Fourth Street
CINCINNATI.O.
PIKES
Opera House Building.

The routes of the street cars are given below. The fare is six cents to any part of the city, with the exception of Mount Auburn.

CINCINNATI STREET R. R.

ROUTE.—Cars start from the corner of Fourth and Vine Streets; thence north on Vine to Seventh Street; thence west on Seventh to Freeman; thence north on Freeman to Hamilton road; thence (returning) south on Freeman to York Street; thence east on York to Linn; thence south on Lynn to Ninth Street; thence east on Ninth to Walnut; thence south on Walnut to Fourth; thence west on Fourth to Vine Street.

CITY PASSENGER STREET R. R.

Office, north-west corner Fourth and Main Streets. ROUTE. —Cars start from the intersection of Fourth and Main Streets; thence west on Fourth to John; thence north on John to Findlay; thence west on Findlay to Baymiller; thence north on Baymiller to Bank Street; thence west on Bank Street to Patterson; thence north on Patterson to Harrison pike; thence east on Harrison pike to Cumminsville pike; thence (returning) south on Central Avenue to Fifth Street; thence east on Fifth to Main; thence south on Main to place of beginning.

PASSENGER STREET R. R.

Office, north-west corner Fourth and Main Streets. ROUTE. —Cars start from the corner of Third and Lawrence Streets; thence north on Lawrence to Fourth; thence west on Fourth to Smith; thence north on Smith to Fifth; thence west on Fifth to north-west corner of Fifth and Freeman; thence (returning) east on Fifth, by double track, to Wood Street; thence south on Wood to Third; thence east on Third to place of beginning.

PENDLETON STREET R. R.

Office, north-west corner Third and Lock Streets. ROUTE No. 5 commences at Fourth and Walnut; up Walnut to Fifth;

east on Fifth to Broadway; south on Broadway to Pearl; east on Pearl to junction with Front Street at Little Miami Depot; thence east on Front to Washington, the terminus—returning by Third and Martin Streets to Pearl; west on Pearl to Broadway; up Broadway to Fourth; west on Fourth to Walnut. ROUTE No. 7 commences at Washington Street, terminus of Route No. 5; thence east on Front Street to Sportsman's Hall and Ohmer's Garden—returning, by double track, to Washington Street. Distance from Fourth and Walnut to Sportsman's Hall, four and one-fourth miles; time, every six minutes. The cars on this road pass the Little Miami Depot and the Dry Docks and ship-yards of Fulton. Steam cars every fifteen minutes from Ohmer's Garden to Columbia; also Horse-cars from Miami Depot, along Front Street, to the Suspension Bridge, connecting with all trains on the Little Miami Road. To Fourth and Walnut daily, four-horse cars connect with each train on Miami Road.

COVINGTON CITY RAILWAY.

Office, Thirteenth and Madison, Covington. ROUTE No. 2.—From Cincinnati side of Suspension Bridge to Second Street; on Second to Scott; on Scott to Third; on Third to Madison; thence to Eighteenth Street; return the same route to Third and Scott; thence on Third to Greenup; on Greenup to Second; on Second to Bridge; and across the Bridge to Cincinnati.

STORRS AND SEDAMSVILLE STREET R. R.

Cars leave Sedamsville, going east, at 6 A. M., and every fifteen minutes thereafter, during the day, up to 7 P. M. Leave foot of Sixth, going west, at 6:30 A. M., and every fifteen minutes thereafter, during the day. Night car leaves Sedamsville at 7, 8, 9, and 10 P. M., going east—and foot of Sixth Street at 7:30, 8:30, 9:30, and 10:30 P. M., going west. The line of this road commences at foot of Sixth Street, and runs along the River road, through Sedamsville, to Readersville, a distance of three miles.

CUMMINSVILLE AND SPRING GROVE R. R.

Offices, Gate No. 1, Spring Grove Avenue, and at Cumminsville. Cars leave Benkenstein's Garden every ten minutes,

running on Spring Grove Avenue to Cumminsville and Spring Grove Cemetery. Distance, two miles from Cincinnati to Cumminsville; do., three miles to Spring Grove Cemetery—returning same route every ten minutes. Last car leaves Benkenstein's at 11 P. M. Fare to Cumminsville, ten cents; to Spring Grove, fifteen cents. Cars start at 6 A. M.; connect with John Street and Freeman Street Lines. Depot, one square from Brighton House. Strangers wishing to visit Spring Grove Cemetery can procure tickets at the office of Secretary Samuel B. Spear, Pike's Opera House, up stairs, or at the first toll-gate on the road.

MT. AUBURN AND CINCINNATI STREET R. R.

Office, 232 Main Street. ROUTE.—From Fifth, up Main, to Orchard; thence to Sycamore—returning on Liberty, Main, Court, and Walnut Streets. Time, every fifteen minutes. From corner Sycamore and Liberty, cars ascend the hill to Mount Auburn; return same route. Time, thirty minutes. First car down, 6 A. M.; last car up, 9:15 P. M.

FIRE-ALARM STATIONS.

The number of the box signaling the fire will be struck upon the bells of all the engine houses, together with that upon the Mechanics Institute. For example: To announce an alarm from signal box No. 24, the bells will be struck TWICE, and after a pause of five seconds, will be struck FOUR times: thus, 2—4. If from No. 124, thus, 1—2—4. The number of the box will be repeated at intervals of twenty seconds until a sufficient alarm has been sounded.

LIST OF SIGNAL BOXES.

1. Eng. House No. 15, Observatory and Pavilion Sts.
2. Fifth and Elm.
3. Cent. Avenue and Sixth.
4. Eng. House No. 14, Fifth near Smith.

5. Third and Smith.
6. Second and John.
7. Front and Smith.
8. John and Clark.
9. Front and Elm.
12. Engine House No. 1, Race and Commerce.
13. Walnut and Second.
14. Front and Main.
15. Second and Sycamore.
16. Front and Broadway.
17. Front and Pike.
18. Little Miami R. R. Depot, west end.
19. Engine House No. 6, Pearl and Martin.
21. Third and Lock.
23. Fifth and Lock.
24. Eng. House No. 10, Third and Lawrence.
25. Market and East Front (Drug Store).
26. Main and Pearl.
27. Third and Vine.
28. Third and Elm.
29. I. & C. R. R. Depot, Pearl and Plum.
31. Fourth and Central Ave.
32. Fourth and Race.
34. Fourth and Walnut.
35. Vine and Water.
36. Sixth and Main.
37. Fifth and Sycamore.
38. Sixth and Broadway.
39. Eighth and Miami Canal.
41. Eng. House No. 4, Sycamore and Whetstone Al.
42. Eighth and Walnut.
43. Seventh and Race.
45. Ninth and Elm.
46. Marine Railway, Fulton.
47. Eighth and Mound.
48. Seventh and Cutter.
49. Sixth and Park.
51. Eng. House No. 2, Ninth and Freeman.
52. Seventh and Baymiller.
53. Sixth and Baymiller.
54. Fifth & I. & C. R. R. B'dge.
56. Fourth and Mill.
57. Front and Mill.
58. Wood and Front.
59. Sixth and Freeman.
61. Sixth and Harriet.
62. Sixth and Front.
63. Eighth and Harriet.
64. Gest and Harriet.
65. Richmond and Linn.
67. Court and Cutter.
68. Richmond and John.
69. Plum and South Canal.
71. Eng. House No. 5, Vine, north of Court.
72. Twelfth and Race.
73. Twelfth and Walnut.
74. Court and Main.
75. Eighth & Accommodat'n.
76. Hunt and Broadway.
78. Sycamore and Abigail.
79. Spring and Woodward.
81. Eng. House No. 7, Webster, bet. Main and Sycamore.
82. Liberty and Pendleton.
83. Junction of Lebanon and Montgomery Roads.
84. North Mount Auburn.
85. Mason St., Mt. Auburn.
86. Sycamore and Schiller.
87. Mulberry and Locust.
89. Vine and Mulberry.
91. Eng. House No. 12, Hamilton Road and Vine.
92. Walnut and Liberty.
93. Walnut and Mercer.

BANK OF DISCOUNT AND DEPOSIT.
Espy, Heidelbach & Co.
S. E. Cor. 3rd & Vine St.
Cincinnati.
Dealers in Foreign Exchange.

94. Race and Fourteenth.
95. Vine and Milk.
96. Elm and Liberty.
97. Elm and Findlay.
98. Hamilton Road and Elm.
121. Eng. House No. 13, Bank, bet. Cent. Ave. & Linn.
123. Central Ave. and York.
124. Linn and York.
125. Poplar and Linn.
126. Central Ave. & Liberty.
127. John and Wade.
128. Central Ave. & Clinton.
129. East end of Seventeenth Ward.
131. Eng. House No. 8, Cutter, bet. Laurel and Betts.
132. Linn and Clark.
134. Baymiller and Laurel.
135. Freeman and Hopkins.
136. Freeman and Everett.
137. Linn and Everett.
138. Baymiller and Liberty.
139. Freeman and Findlay.
141. Freeman and Bank.
142. Cent. Ave. & Baymiller.
143. Brighton House.
145. Brighton St. & Cent. Ave
146. Third and Coliard.
147. Ninth St. Police Station
148. Bremen St. Police Stat'n
149. Fulton Police Station.
151. Hammond St. Police St'n.
152. Cent. Ave. Police Station.
153. Little Miami Locomotive Works.
154. John and Water.
156. Harrison Road, west of Millcreek Bridge.
157. Eng. House No. 11, East Front and Vance.
158. Farmers Hotel, Fulton.
161. Central Station, Sixth and Vine.
162. Front, west of Millcreek
163. Gest, west of Millcreek.
164. Western Ave. and Bank.
165. Fourteenth and Race.
171. Walnut Hills.
172. Work-house.

Cincinnati has five railroad depots, including one in Covington, which are used by thirteen different lines. These are designated as follows:

Dayton Depot, Hoadly Street, between Fifth and Sixth Streets.

Covington Depot, Eighth and Washington Streets, Covington.

Indianapolis Depot, Plum and Pearl Streets.

Little Miami Depot, Kilgour and Front Streets.

Ohio and Mississippi Depot, West Front Street, corner of Mill Street.

The ticket offices can be found under the Burnet House.

The following tables will give the chief lines of railway leading out of Cincinnati, with principal intermediate and connecting points, and names of general officers in Cincinnati.

CINCINNATI, HAMILTON AND DAYTON R. R.

Connecting for Richmond, Connersville, Rushville, Cambridge City, Dayton, Lima, Fort Wayne, Chicago and the North-west; Sandusky, Cleveland, and Buffalo, Toledo, Detroit, and all Points in Canada. (Dayton Depot.)

D. McLaren, *General Superintendent.*
Samuel Stevenson, *General Ticket Agent.*

CINCINNATI AND ZANESVILLE R. R.

Morrow, Wilmington, Circleville. (Little Miami Depot.)

ERIE AND ATLANTIC AND GREAT WESTERN R. R.

One thousand two hundred and fifty miles under one management; eight hundred and sixty miles without change of coaches. The entire Broad-Guage Line from

The Poor Man's Wealth!
The Rich Man's Best Investment!

MUTUAL BENEFIT
LIFE INSURANCE CO.

OF NEWARK, N. J.

ASSETS OVER - - $18,000,000.

At the age of 30 an Estate of

$20,000,

Free of incumbrance, and under the laws of Ohio not liable
for debt, is secured by the annual payment of $236 00, with
small interest on order, the dividends paying the order

$15,000

By payment of $177 00, in like manner.

$10,000

By payment of $118 00, in like manner.

$5,000

By payment of $59 00, in like manner.

$2,500

By payment of $29 50, in like manner.

Other ages, from **14** to **65** years, at proportionate rates.

This Company has been Established in Cincinnati 25 years.

Apply to   **ROB'T SIMPSON**, State Agent,

Office S. E. Cor. Walnut and Third Sts.,

CINCINNATI.

Cincinnati to New York has been consolidated, and is now managed and operated by the Erie Company.

The track has been put in the most perfect condition, and the equipment of the line greatly improved. (Dayton Depot.)

W. B. Shattuc, *Passenger Agent.*

CINCINNATI AND INDIANAPOLIS JUNCTION R. R.

For Oxford, Connersville, Cambridge City, Newcastle, Rushville, Indianapolis, Terre Haute, St. Louis, and all points West. (Dayton Depot.)

J. H. Sheldon, *Superintendent.*

J. A. Perkins, *General Freight Agent.*

INDIANAPOLIS, CINCINNATI AND LAFAYETTE R. R.

Through passenger route from Cincinnati to St. Louis, Chicago, Cairo, Memphis, New Orleans, Springfield, Quincy, St. Joseph, Keokuk, Des Moines, Omaha, and all towns and cities in the West, North-west, and South-west. (Indianapolis Depot.)

The splendid Passenger Depot of the I. C. & L. R. R. is about a mile nearer the business center of the city than the depot of any other railroad, and within a few squares of the Post-office and the principal hotels and steamboat landings.

J. F. Richardson, *Superintendent.*

A. E. Clark, *General Ticket Agent.*

LITTLE MIAMI RAILROAD, VIA COLUMBUS.

Elegant Silver Palace day and sleeping cars combined, are run through from Cincinnati to New York without change. This is the famous Pan-Handle route. The morning express goes through to New York in twenty-nine hours. Express train leaves every night. Trains run by Columbus time, which is seven minutes faster than Cincinnati time.

W. L. O'Brien, *General Ticket Agent.*

D. G. A. Davenport, *Auditor.*

LOUISVILLE AND CINCINNATI R. R.

Just completed; an air line to Louisville, 106 miles. This will, in time, connect with the new railroad bridge. (Covington Depot.)

KENTUCKY CENTRAL R. R.

Covington, Cynthiana, Paris, Lexington. (Covington Depot.)

H. P. Ransom, *General Ticket Agent.*

MARIETTA AND CINCINNATI R. R.

Loveland, Chillicothe, Athens. (Indianapolis Depot.)
C. F. Low, *General Ticket Agent.*

OHIO AND MISSISSIPPI R. R.

Three daily express trains leave Cincinnati, arriving at St. Louis in about twelve hours, and connecting with West-bound express trains for Quincy, St. Joseph,

Leavenworth, Kansas City, **Lawrence, and all** Western points; connecting at Odin, without delay, **with** the Illinois Central for Cairo, Memphis, Mobile, New Orleans, and all Southern points; and connecting at Sandoval for Galena, Dubuque, and all parts of the North-west.

One train, Sunday evening, through to Louisville, St. Louis, and Cairo. Depot, foot of Mill Street.

A. H. Lewis, *General Superintendent.*

C. E. Follett, *General Passenger Agent.*

UNITED STATES MAIL LINE STEAMERS

to Madison and Louisville. From wharf-boat, foot of Vine Street, at 12 M., Major Anderson, Captain Samuel Hildreth; General Buell, Captain Charles David, landing for all way business. The splendid steamers, General Lytle, Captain R. M. Wade; St. Charles, Captain David Whitten, leave foot of Vine Street at 5:30 P. M., landing at Aurora and Madison only.

On Sundays only one boat, departing at 12 M., making all mail landings. All these steamers make prompt connection at Louisville with morning trains for Nashville, Memphis, and all points South. Through railroad tickets, between Cincinnati and Louisville, will be received for passage on these steamers, and will entitle the holder to meals and state-room free. Baggage checked to all principal points on the boats.

C. G. Pearce, *President.* Thos. Sherlock, *Treasurer.*

To all points upon the Ohio and the great system of rivers of the Mississippi Valley steamers may be found at the levee.

The various stage lines out of the city are given in the Directory.

The Express offices are located as follows:

Adams Express, 67 West Fourth Street; J. H. Rhodes, Agent.

American Express, 118 West Fourth Street; Frank Clark, Agent.

Harnden Express, 114 West Third Street; D. F. Raymond, Agent.

United States Express, 122 West Fourth Street; J. J. Henderson, Agent.

The suburbs of Cincinnati are so essentially a part of the city—their population having entire community of interest with the residents of the city proper—that a detailed description of them, in addition to allusions already made, would seem to have proper place in these pages. But to do justice to them would transcend the limits of this summary view, and the briefest mention only is here made, while the reader is referred to the interesting volume prepared by Sidney D. Maxwell, Esq., in which their beauties and attractions are fully set forth. They are a sylvan crown adorning the brow of the Queen of the West.

AVONDALE

is a little **east of north of the center of the city, at a** distance of two miles **and a half. Here are to be found the quiet** and simple **pleasures of rural life, remote** from **any thing to suggest the crowded, noisy, dusty city. The population of this village is not far from twelve** hundred, and embraces **many** of the well-known citizens of Cincinnati.

CLIFTON

is the pride **of Cincinnati. Its park-like grounds, its** beautiful drives, **its magnificent prospects, its splendid** residences, make it **a chief point of interest to** tourists. Its charming retirement **has been invaded by nothing** in the shape **of shop or store. Residences are here of palatial** elegance **and size, and surroundings which present every thing beautiful which taste and wealth** can furnish.

COLLEGE HILL,

is five miles from the city limits, in a north-westerly direction. It is the seat of two widely-known institutions—Farmers College **and the Ohio Female College. The** Presbyterians **and Episcopalians have excellent houses of worship. Within this village is one of the** highest **points of land in Hamilton County. Good** schools, the **best social elements, and religious privileges** are the features of College Hill.

EAST WALNUT HILLS

is a little over three miles north-east of the Court-house in Cincinnati, and adjoins the village of Wood-burn. Here are some of the finest residences in the vicinity of the city, and landscape views which, in their variety and beauty, have no superior upon the Hudson or the Rhine. Hills, dales, and river combine to present to the eye a feast of which it never tires.

GLENDALE

is one of the most delightful suburban villages in the United States. It is north of Cincinnati, fifteen miles by rail and twelve by turnpike. The Glendale Female College is located here. The Presbyterians, Swedenborgians, and Episcopalians have flourishing churches, and the public school is of the first class. The quiet beauty and social advantages of this place are well known, and the evidences of taste, refinement, and wealth visible on every hand.

MOUNT AUBURN

is now almost wholly within the city limits. It has long enjoyed the reputation of being one of the chief attractions of Cincinnati. Residents here have all the enjoyment of rural life, at the same time being within easy reach of all the advantages which the city can offer. Several of the public charitable institutions are

FOR

MONUMENTS

OF

POLISHED GRANITE,

MARBLE AND PORPHYRY,

APPLY TO

JAMES G. BATTERSON,

HARTFORD, CONN.,

IN PERSON OR BY LETTER.

DESIGNS AND ESTIMATES FORWARDED BY MAIL OR
EXPRESS TO ALL PARTS OF THE COUNTRY.

MANY OF THE

FINEST MONUMENTS

IN SPRING GROVE CEMETERY

WERE FROM THIS ESTABLISHMENT,

WHICH IMPORTS DIRECT FROM

SCOTLAND, FRANCE, NORWAY, SWEDEN, RUSSIA, FINLAND AND ITALY,

THE MOST BEAUTIFUL

GRANITES AND MARBLES

IN THE WORLD.

located here, and the Mount Auburn Ladies' Institute affords unsurpassed educational facilities.

WALNUT HILLS,

now partly within the city limits, has long been famous as the seat of Lane Theological Seminary. A settlement was made here in 1791. It is easily accessible, and offers in its educational and religious advantages, one of the most desirable localities for residences in the neighborhood of Cincinnati.

WOODBURN

embraces about a section of land, and is two miles north-east of the Court-house in Cincinnati. Many of its beautiful building sites command extensive prospects of the most charming description. The village is controlled by a class of citizens whose administration contributes every thing necessary to its beauty and the comfort of the residents.

WYOMING,

about two miles south of Glendale, twelve miles from Cincinnati by rail, is a delightful suburb. Some of its building sites are unsurpassed in beauty, and command extensive views up and down the Millcreek valley, upon which the eye never ceases to dwell with pleasure.

Of other suburbs of Cincinnati which present many

points of rural beauty, Mount Washington, Linwood, Oakley, Fairmount, Spring Grove, Mount Harrison, Glen Grove, Riverside, Mount Airy, Mahketewah, and Hartwell, only the names can be here given.

A summary view has now been taken of the attractions and advantages of Cincinnati, both as a place of trade and residence, with a glance at its institutions and internal improvements.

The comparison of its area with that of other Western cities, which are spread over a much larger territory, will show how much greater it will be, in statistics of population, when, like them, it embraces within municipal limits all adjacent settled localities. Annexation is already the progressive watchword, and erelong the area will be largely increased.

The City moves forward in the steady march of improvement, and Public Spirit points to the magnificent possibilities of coming years. Who shall define the limits of Cincinnati at its centennial, or calculate its increase in all the elements of a wealthy, populous, and powerful municipality?

RESOR'S BLOCK.

THE MOUNT AUBURN

Young Ladies' Institute.

Established 1856.

The advantages of this School are:

1. Its Location.—Within the city limits, it is only a half hour's drive distant from any of the Depots, and within easy call of the Telegraph Offices. Post-office, and Stores. But being five hundred feet above the level of the river, it has none of the annoyances of the city. Surrounded by beautiful residences, it looks out in every direction upon a delightful prospect, and is as free from intrusion as though it were in a quiet country village.

2. Its Home Influence.—The building used by the Boarding Department is entirely detached from the School House. Its rooms, each of which is designed to accommodate two young ladies, are large, and are furnished with a view to make them home-like. A Parlor, 50 by 40 feet, is devoted exclusively to the school. The discipline of the School is that of the family. It is the constant aim of those in charge to keep up the home feeling, to create an atmosphere of perfect *material* comfort, and then to administer a moral discipline inspired by love, and instructed by the law of Christ.

3. Its Extended and Comprehensive Course of Study.—The course of study runs through three departments, of four years each, insuring a continuous and symmetrical mental discipline. The length of the course guarantees comprehensiveness. The classical schedule comprises a list of the higher branches of study, which bears comparison with that of colleges for young men.

4. The QUALITY of its Instruction.—No Instructors are employed but those who have either, by long experience, proved themselves apt to teach, or who have been trained in the School. To secure such, no expense has been spared.

☞ *For further information, address,*

I. H. WHITE, Treasurer,
or **Rev. A. J. ROWLAND, President,**

CINCINNATI.

The Cincinnati Chronicle,

DAILY AND WEEKLY,

IS A FIRST-CLASS

Political and Family Newspaper.

Political Principles.

In politics the Chronicle is Republican, but not partisan; never neutral, but always independent. Adhering to the principles of that great party under whose auspices the gallant soldiers of the Republic were led and cheered to victory over treason and armed rebellion, it none the less freely and independently discusses all political measures proposed for public sanction, presenting the claims of party only as a means of promoting the good of the whole country.

Home and Foreign News.

As a news center for the entire Mississippi Valley, Cincinnati has no superior, and has facilities which defy competition from even the great commercial centers of the East. The latest news from all parts of the world to the hour of going to press, will be given from two days to one week in advance of the Eastern weeklies. The news from Europe by the ocean cable is published at the same moment in Cincinnati as in New York.

Literature, Science, and Art.

For the general reader we shall give each week a digested summary of Personal Items, Literary Intelligence, Notices of New Books and Magazines, Scientific Developments and Discoveries in Art. With each number will be given one or more domestic stories suited to the home circle.

Official Paper of City and County.

No newspaper ever started under as favorable auspices as the Chronicle. In the short space of twelve months, so popular had it become with the people, and so successful its management, that it was made *the official paper*, for doing both City and County advertising.

Advertising in the Chronicle.

The very large and rapidly-growing circulation of both the Daily and the Weekly Chronicle, throughout the whole West, renders them unsurpassed as mediums of advertising. Communications from the business public in regard to rates, etc., will receive prompt attention.

Address, **CHRONICLE COMPANY,**

CINCINNATI, OHIO.

T.W. SPRAGUE & CO.
CUSTOM TAILORING & FINE CLOTHING READY MADE.
MEN'S YOUTHS & BOYS CLOTHING
T.W. SPRAGUE & CO.
83
S.E. Corner Fourth & Vine. Sts. Cincinnati.

THE CINCINNATI GAZETTE:

DAILY, SEMI-WEEKLY, AND WEEKLY.

As a newspaper, the Daily Gazette is not surpassed by any publication in the United States. It covers the entire field of News, Literature, Commerce, Manufactures, Agriculture, and Amusements, and occupies it fully. Matter coming under these heads, not found in the Gazette, will not be worth reading. In its Editorial Department, the Gazette has all the excellence that a variety of first-class talent can impart to it.

TERMS OF THE DAILY:

By mail, per annum...$12.00
   do.   for six months..6.00

THE SEMI-WEEKLY GAZETTE.

This paper is printed on Tuesday and Friday of each week. It is the same size of the Daily and Weekly, containing thirty-six full columns of reading matter. Most of the reading matter prepared for the Daily and Weekly will be printed in this edition. Persons who desire a paper oftener than once a week, but do not need a daily, will find this the cheapest and best paper published anywhere.

TERMS OF THE SEMI-WEEKLY:

One copy (104 Nos.)...$4.00

An extra copy will be sent to the getter up of each club of ten and upward.

The Weekly Gazette contains more reading matter than any other newspaper published in the United States. Having no great political battles to fight during the year, we shall have more space for general and miscellaneous reading. This will be occupied, in part, by articles under the head of **PERSONAL RECOLLECTIONS**, one of which will be published weekly. These will be written by eminent men in various parts of the West, who have already been engaged for that purpose. Our authors have been selected from the various professions, including Ministers, Lawyers, Politicians, Farmers, Merchants, and Editors. Each article will have attached to it the name of the writer. The gentlemen whose services have been secured occupy high positions, and have made for themselves national reputations.

Other Departments, including Editorial, News, Commercial, Correspondence, Agricultural, and Miscellaneous, will be carried to the standard of excellence. Important news transpiring at home or abroad will be published in the Gazette from three to six days in advance of Eastern publications.

TERMS OF THE WEEKLY:

One copy $2.00

ADDRESS

GAZETTE COMPANY,
CINCINNATI.

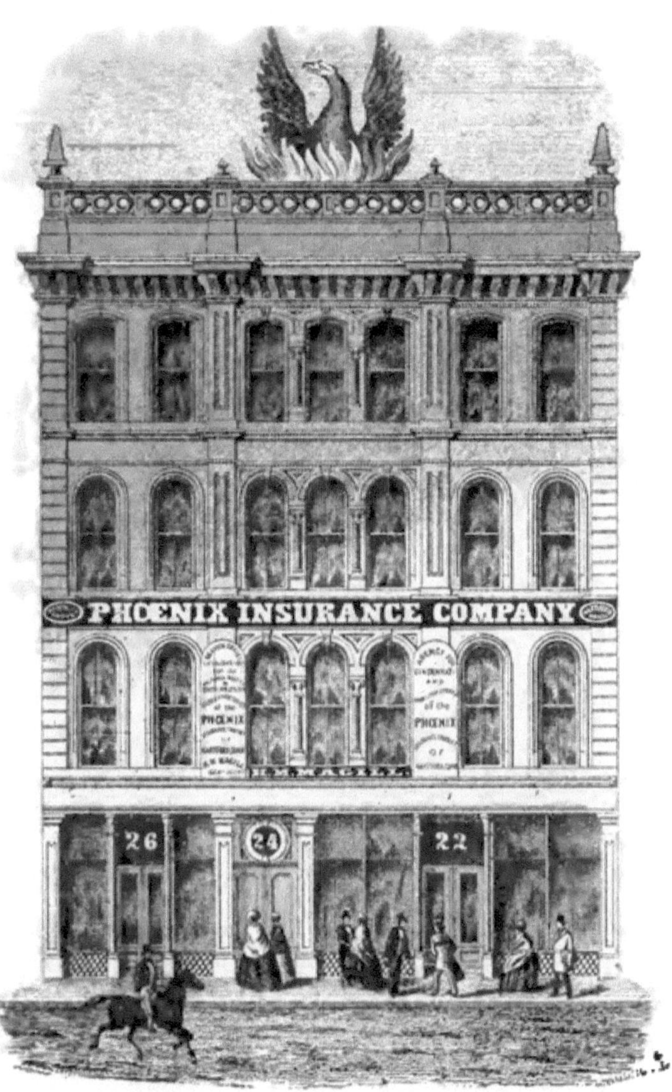

PHŒNIX INSURANCE COMPANY
26
24
22

Appletons' Journal.

APPLETONS' JOURNAL is published weekly. It consists of thirty-two quarto pages, each number illustrated, or accompanied by a Pictorial Supplement. It is devoted to popular current Literature, an organ of advanced opinion with respect to all the great interests of society, of popular Science in its best sense, and of Art.

The department of Literature embraces Fiction, in the form of both serial novels and short stories; Essays upon literary and social topics; Sketches of travel and adventure; Discussions upon art, books, and kindred themes; Papers upon all the various subjects that pertain to the pursuits and recreations of the people, whether of town or country; and Poems by our foremost poets.

A distinctive feature is a fuller treatment of Science than is prevalent in popular journals. In this branch the publishers have secured the services of the ablest and most authoritative thinkers.

Illustrations form an important feature in the plan of the JOURNAL. They usually consist of either an Illustrated Supplement on some popular theme, a Steel Engraving in the best style of the art, or a large Cartoon engraved on wood—those on steel, and the cartoons, consisting of views of American scenery by our most distinguished painters.

D. APPLETON & CO., NEW YORK.

Price 10 Cents per No., or $4.00 per Annum, in advance.

PUTNAM'S MONTHLY MAGAZINE

OF

LITERATURE, SCIENCE, ART,

AND

NATIONAL INTERESTS.

PUTNAM'S MAGAZINE will be a National publication, supported by the best writers, in each department, from every section of the country. High-toned papers on matters of National Interest, Popular Science, Industrial Pursuits, and sound Information and Instruction on important topics, will be especially cultivated. In the lighter articles, Healthy Entertainment and Pure Amusement for the family circle will be carefully chosen from the ample resources presented by a large circle of contributors.

TERMS.—$4.00 *per Annum in advance, or 35 Cents per Number.*

Special premiums for clubs.

G. P. PUTNAM & SON, PUBLISHERS,
661 BROADWAY, NEW YORK.

Cincinnati, Hamilton and Dayton R. R. Depot.

CARLISLE BUILDING

Franklin Insurance Co.

OF CINCINNATI.

Office, No. 96 West Third Street, Cincinnati.

Cash Capital, ... $150,000 00
Surplus, Jan. 1, 1869, ... 40,309 16
                                    —————————
                                    $190,309 16

Directors:

John S. Taylor,	Wm. Glenn,	Alexander Swift,
Samuel Davis, Jr.,	G. S. Blanchard,	Lewis Wald,
Caleb Allen,	M. Fechheimer,	J. Stacey Hill.

JOHN S. TAYLOR, President.

C. E. DEMAREST, Secretary.
J. A. KEY, Surveyor·

☞ Fire and Marine Policies issued on favorable terms. Insures Buildings, Merchandise, **Furniture, Rents, Leases,** etc., against loss or damage by fire.

ELM STREET PRINTING COMPANY,

176 & 178 Elm Street,

CINCINNATI, OHIO.

The effort of the Editors and Publishers of the Religious Journals of this city, to build up a first-class Printing Establishment, has been so far successful that they have erected another five-story brick building in addition to that occupied in 1868.

The policy of *charging low prices* has been vindicated by our experience thus far, as profitable to the Company and satisfactory to our patrons.

Our Book and Jobbing Departments are liberally supplied with all that is requisite to execute large amounts of work neatly, tastefully, and promptly.

Orders for Pamphlets, Books, Stereotyping; Commercial, Bank, and Railroad Printing, etc., will receive prompt attention.

☞ *We will give satisfaction* in all cases to those favoring us with orders.

Estimates carefully made for those proposing to print books, pamphlets, or other work. *Address*

W. C. GRAY,

Treasurer and Superintendent.

CINCINNATI WEEKLY TIMES.

Established in 1843.

This paper, in its enlarged and improved condition, is well known as the largest and cheapest weekly paper now published in the Western country, if not in the United States. The following is a list of the number of post-offices in the different States to which it is sent:

Ohio	1616	Virginia	250
Tennessee	200	Michigan	361
Iowa	623	Kentucky	289
Wisconsin	610	New York	416
Kansas	140	Pennsylvania	671
Illinois	970	Minnesota	90
Indiana	800	Other States	3000
Missouri	367		

Thus it will be seen that the WEEKLY TIMES is circulated through more than *ten thousand post-offices*, and, from this fact, affords an excellent medium for those who wish to advertise their business.

TERMS.—*Single subscriptions, $2.00 per year; Clubs of Ten, $1.50 each, an extra copy to getter up of the Club.*

ADVERTISING IN WEEKLY TIMES:

As Ordinary Advertisements .... 50 Cents per line, each insertion
As Special Notices .... 75 " " " " "
As Reading Matter ....$1 00 " " " "

Circulation, 67,000 Weekly.

Cincinnati Daily Times.

Established by the Present Proprietor in 1840.

City Subscribers supplied by Carriers at 20 Cents per Week.

Mail Subscribers, $8.00 per Year.

This is the oldest Daily Paper (with one exception) in Cincinnati. Having been for many years the *only Evening Paper* in the city, and being read by all classes, the TIMES can claim a large and increasing circulation.

It is particularly adapted to the *family circle*, from its well-selected news, its instructive and interesting miscellany, its moral sketches, etc., etc.

The *telegraphic news* from all quarters, up to 4 o'clock of each afternoon, will be found, as usual, in the columns of the TIMES.

From its compact form, and the manner in which it is made up—having reading matter on each page, thereby allowing advertisements in every part of the paper to be readily seen—in addition to its *large circulation*, not only in the city, but in the adjoining towns, the TIMES must continue to be a most desirable *medium for advertisers.*

ADVERTISING IN DAILY TIMES:

One Square, each insertion, inside (space of Ten Lines, seven words to the line).. $0.75
One Square, One Month, First Page... 12.00
One Square, One Month, Fourth Page....................................... 8.00

C. W. STARBUCK & CO.,
No. 62 West Third Street, Cincinnati, O.

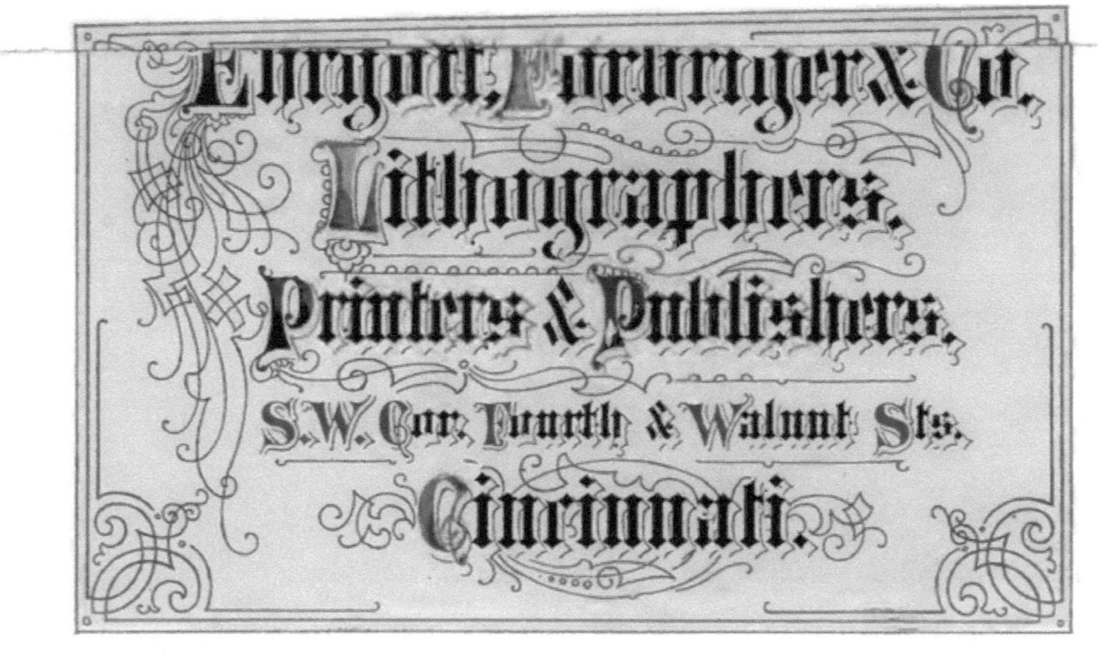
Ehrgott, Forbriger & Co.,
Lithographers,
Printers & Publishers,
S.W. Cor. Fourth & Walnut Sts.
Cincinnati.

Stiff
Lithographic
Printing House.
Ehrgott, Forbriger & Co.
Lithographers,
Printers & Publishers,
S. W. Cor. Fourth & Walnut Sts.
Cincinnati.

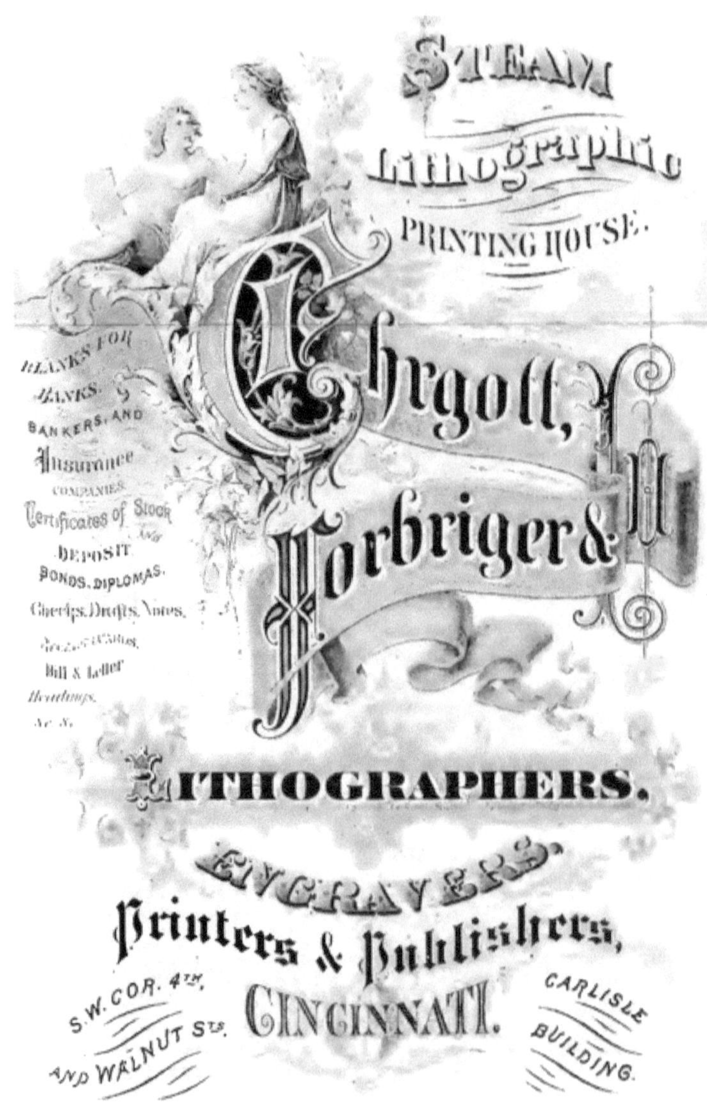

STEAM
Lithographic
PRINTING HOUSE.
Ehrgott,
Forbriger &
BLANKS FOR
BANKS.
BANKERS, AND
Insurance
COMPANIES
Certificates of Stock
AND
DEPOSIT
BONDS, DIPLOMAS.
Checks, Drafts, Notes.
Bill & Letter
Headings.
&c. &c.
LITHOGRAPHERS.
ENGRAVERS,
Printers & Publishers,
S.W. COR. 4TH,
AND WALNUT STS.
CINCINNATI.
CARLISLE
BUILDING.

STEAM
Lithographic
PRINTING HOUSE.